SAVED FOR BEN:

THE LEGACY

JACQUELYN B. SMITH

WestBow Press books may be ordered through booksellers or by contacting:

WestBow Press
A Division of Thomas Nelson & Zondervan
1663 Liberty Drive
Bloomington, IN 47403
www.westbowpress.com
844-714-3454

ISBN: 978-1-6642-6896-8 (sc)
ISBN: 978-1-6642-6898-2 (hc)
ISBN: 978-1-6642-6897-5 (e)

Library of Congress Control Number: 2022911128

Print information available on the last page.

WestBow Press rev. date: 07/12/2022

This *Saved for Ben* series is dedicated to my loving and nurturing grandmother, Ora Lee Woods; a second to none mother, Lillie Mae Wood; and my village. My grandmother and mother used every opportunity available to broaden my horizons and instill life changing godly principles in me.

God has connected wonderful people to my journey of spiritual growth. My village consists of those who have prayed, encouraged, and helped me during my journey of academic years, military service, and personal growth whether in Georgia, Virginia, Texas, or Florida. I am forever grateful for their love, support, and endearing friendship. Last but now least, to my son, Jeremy, a precious gift of God, who has inspired me to continue making a difference through writing for those who are willing to trust God.

CONTENTS

1

WELCOME HOME

After enjoying three weeks in Atlanta, Ben and Wanda returned from their honeymoon on Sunday afternoon. After another night of beautiful lovemaking with her husband, Wanda was unpacking the suitcases from their wonderful honeymoon and getting all of her film together to drop off at the drug store so it could be developed.

She looked at Ben and said, "I'm so happy Ben!"

Ben said, "I am too! I wake up with a smile on my face. I love the way you snuggle up to me when you sleep."

Wanda laughed and asked, "Am I sleeping too close to you?"

Ben said, "No, I love it!"

Wanda said, "I love being close to you. I feel such peace. I slept better in the last few weeks than I have ever slept in my life."

Ben said, "I have too! I have a sense of completion with you. I guess, you complete me."

Wanda laughed.

Ben said, "However, because of you I'm also more alert of our surroundings. I want to make sure you're safe."

Wanda smiled.

Ben said, "Well, we need to make our rounds and let everyone know that we're back!"

Wanda said, "I know. Let's go by your mother's house first, then we can stop by the store."

Ben said, "That's a plan. Do you want to go for a run first?"

Wanda said, "Normally, I would. However, after last night and this morning, I don't need to work out!"

Ben laughed!

It was around ten o'clock in the morning when Ben and Wanda parked the car in front of his mom's house. Mom's car and David's truck were parked on the street.

As Ben walked into his childhood home, he asked, "Is anyone home?"

Mom rushed to hug her son and new daughter in law. His siblings, Mary and David, did the same.

Mom said, "We were wondering when you would get back."

Mary said, "I knew you would stay at least three weeks."

Smiling Wanda said, "Yeah, two weeks was just not enough."

David asked, "How was Atlanta? Amazing isn't it?"

Ben said, "It was fantastic. We had a great time."

Mary asked, "Where did you stay?"

Wanda said, "We stayed at a condo. It's beautiful. I can't wait for you to see it."

Confused Mom asked, "See it?"

Ben said, "Yes, I made an investment and bought the condo last month for our honeymoon."

Wanda said, "We will need the space when David graduates from culinary school."

David asked, "Which side of town is it on?"

Ben said, “It’s near downtown. We could walk to a lot of restaurants and shops.”

Impressed David said, “That was a good investment!”

Mary said, “Hopefully, we won’t have to wait until David graduates to go visit.”

Ben said, “No, I’m sure we can drive up and spend the weekend there soon!”

Mom said, “Well, while you were in Atlanta, we missed you!”

Wanda said, “We missed you too. That’s why we only stayed three weeks!”

Everyone laughed.

Mary said, “I was just telling Mom that I need a car during my senior year.”

Mom said, “I told her, Dad left her the money to purchase a car when she graduates.”

Mary said, “I can’t wait until then. I’m not being greedy. I’m involved in so many things this year that I need a car to get around. Last year, Ben would drop me off, Wanda would pick me up. You would drop me off and I would find a ride back. I will also be volunteering at the hospital this year.”

Mom exclaimed, “What will you be doing at the hospital?”

Everyone laughed.

Mary said, “I will be serving as an interpreter on call. If a patient does not speak English, but speaks either Spanish or French, they will call me.”

Wanda said, “Wow! Mary, that’s great!”

David said, “That’s one way to keep your language skills up.”

Ben said, “I’m not against you volunteering. I was just wondering; do we have many people in Fairville who don’t speak English?”

Everyone laughed.

Mary said, "I asked the same question. Believe it or not, they have had some patients that spoke only Spanish!"

Surprised Mom said, "I would have never thought that!"

Ben said, "Mom, she has a great point. I'm sure if she could persuade Mr. Jennings that she needed the car now instead of in May. He would release the bank account to her."

David agreed, "I think he would too!"

Mom said, "OK, give him a call and make an appointment, but I have to go with you!"

Mary ran to the phone to make the call.

Ben asked, "David, how's your truck doing? My truck started to give me major problems last year."

David said, "I have been thinking about that too. While you were on your honeymoon, I had to have my truck repaired again."

Ben asked, "Do you need money to buy another one?"

David said, "Thanks for offering, but with all of the catering I have done. I have saved enough money to buy another one. I just can't decide if I want another truck or a car."

Ben suggested, "Well with your catering, you may need a van!"

David said, "I know. So, I don't want to buy a car now and have to purchase a van later!"

Ben asked, "Why don't we just go by the Chevrolet dealership tomorrow and see what they have?"

David smiled and said, "Thanks, I would like that!"

Jubilantly Mary ran back in the room and said, "I have an appointment with Mr. Jennings today at one o'clock in the afternoon. Mom can you make it?"

Mom said, "Yes, I can do one o'clock!"

Mary hugged her mom and ran into her room.

Wanda said, "We plan to give Dee my old car. It will get her around town for the next few years before she goes off to college."

Mom said, "That's a good idea. She's been driving it anyway while you were gone!"

Everyone laughed.

Ben and Wanda said their goodbyes and drove to the store. When they arrived at the store, everyone was happy to see them. The store looked great. Uncle Robert was doing a great job. As they walked into the office, Uncle Robert was on the phone. Allowing him to finish his call, they walked into the break room.

With outstretched arms Uncle Robert walked into the break room and said, "Welcome home!"

Wanda and Ben gave him a hug.

Ben said, "We are glad to be back."

Wanda said, "Sort of! It was hard leaving Atlanta!"

Uncle Robert said, "Well, everything here is going well. We are setting new trends each month for sales. All of the reports are on your desk. All of the employees are doing well. Oh! Joshua brought in one of his friends last week and wanted to know if we had any openings."

Ben laughed and asked, "What did you think of the friend?"

Uncle Robert said, "He definitely needs our help and would improve under our tutelage. He's what Joshua used to be!"

Ben asked, "Did you offer him a job?"

Uncle Robert said, "No, I did not. I wanted to talk to you about it first."

Ben said, "I appreciate that. Wanda, what do you think?"

Wanda said, "Well, I feel that anytime we can help someone we should. Look how Joshua's life has changed since he started working at the store in March. His grades have improved, he's a great worker, and his mother is very pleased with his attitude and behavior."

Uncle Robert said, "Joshua is even talking about going to college."

Ben asked, "Well, now that we have promoted Joshua to do other things. Does Mr. Jones need any help in custodial?"

Uncle Robert said, "I have been scheduling Joshua to not only help in stocking merchandise but also custodial. If we hire, his friend, John, we can start him in custodial."

Ben said, "I think custodial is a great entry position for teenagers. Give John the lecture, just like we gave Joshua. If he seems interested, go ahead and hire him."

Uncle Robert said, "Great. No problem!"

Wanda asked, "How are you and Miss Charlene doing?"

Uncle Robert said, "We're doing great. The idea of marriage is crossing my mind."

Ben said, "That's wonderful!"

Wanda said, "I'm so glad, I really like her."

Uncle Robert said, "I do too. We have been dating now for eight months. I think I will ask her around October of this year!"

Wanda asked, "Why wait?"

Uncle Robert said, "Well, it's almost August, I will play it by ear!"

Everyone laughed.

Ben said, "That's great. As you know I will be resuming my studies at the university. I plan to take three courses in both the fall and spring. That way I can graduate in May of next year."

Uncle Robert said, "That's great!"

Ben said, "Wanda and I also plan to open a sporting goods store in Macon. So, I won't be in the store as much as I would like."

Uncle Robert said, "That's fine, I'll just keep you briefed."

Ben said, "Thanks! Remember, I always planned to make you the manager. I can't run this store and open another one too."

Uncle Robert said, "I'm happy with whatever decision you make."

Ben said, "Well, Wanda and I want you to take the manager position now."

Smiling Uncle Robert asked, "Are you ready?"

Wanda said, "Yes, he is. As he said, we can't open a new store and run this store too."

Ben said, "Remember, I told you I needed someone I could trust. You have exceeded all of my expectations. Thank you!"

Uncle Robert said, "It will be an honor to manage this store. I truly enjoy this work."

Ben said, "Great, well effective three weeks ago. You're the manager of the Fairville Cason's Sporting Goods store!"

Uncle Robert said, "I can't wait to tell Charlene!"

Wanda said, "Ooh! His first thought was Charlene!"

Everyone laughed.

Wanda said, "We want to give Dee my car!"

Uncle Robert said, "That's great. She's been driving it while you were gone anyway!"

Everyone laughed.

Ben and Wanda walked to the court house to see Mr. Hank Jennings, their lawyer. Mr. Jennings was standing in the hallway talking when they walked through the court house doors.

Mr. Jennings said, "Here are the newlyweds! How was Atlanta?"

Ben exclaimed, "It was fantastic!"

Wanda said, "The parts of it that we saw!"

Everyone laughed.

Ben asked, "We just wanted to stop by and say hello. We also have some ideas."

Mr. Jennings said, "Well, I don't have an appointment today until Mary at one o'clock. Do you have time to talk now?"

Wanda laughed and said, "That would be great!"

Ben and Wanda walked into the office and took a seat.

Mr. Jennings said, "We had a great time at the wedding. My wife and father are still talking about it."

Ben said, "I'm glad. We're so thankful for your help."

Mr. Jennings said, "I am glad that we could help! My father said that he wants to renew his license again this year just in case someone needs him."

Ben said, "That's great! I told Wanda everything about what Grandpa left for me!"

Wanda said, "I'm still processing the information!"

Mr. Jennings said, "It's a lot to process. I know that you two will continue to do great things! Wanda, I hope you will attend our bi-weekly meetings."

Wanda smiled and said, "I would love that!"

Ben said, "We want to open another sporting goods store in Macon."

Mr. Jennings said, "That's a great idea. Timothy tells me that this store continues to do better each month."

Ben smiled and said, "Yes, we're very happy. Uncle Robert is doing a great job."

Mr. Jennings asked, "Do you have any ideas about a specific location in Macon?"

Ben said, "No, we don't!"

Mr. Jennings said, "The realty company that we work with in Macon can make some recommendations for property. I will give him a call today. Are you free this week to go look at property?"

Ben said, "Yes, I think we should start this process as soon as we can."

Mr. Jennings said, "OK, today is Monday. So, I will have the realtor set up some viewing for Thursday afternoon. Is that OK?"

Wanda said, "That would be fine!"

Ben said, "We would also like to build an intramural sports complex here in Fairville."

Mr. Jennings said, "Now, that is a great idea. I have a younger brother that lives in Atlanta and he is always talking about the youth intramural sports that they have going on up there!"

Wanda said, "Yes, we think that it will be good for the youth, community, and the store. People will need supplies and equipment to play sports!"

Everyone laughed.

Mr. Jennings said, "Now, she's thinking like a business woman!"

Ben said, "I'm not sure if we have enough existing land to build it."

Mr. Jennings said, "Timothy and I will draft a plan and look for some sites here in Fairville."

Ben said, "Great!"

Mr. Jennings asked, "Do you have any more ideas?"

Wanda said, "Yes, we do. I think this is a good start!"

Mr. Jennings said, "This is a great start! I am so excited that you want to continue to improve Fairville. Everywhere I go I hear someone talking about the store, the event center, and the entertainment complex. You have done so much for Fairville already; however, no one knows it's you!"

Wanda said, "I totally understand why we have to keep it a secret. I do want to live a normal life here."

Mr. Jennings said, "The self-service car wash and the storage unit will both open in four weeks. Ben, those were great ideas."

Ben said, "Thanks! We also want to thank you for sprucing up the house. It is spectacular!"

Mr. Jennings said, "I'm so glad you like it."

Wanda said, "We love it. The new appliances, the paint color, the carpet, and the beautiful flowers. We love it. It was a beautiful sight when we drove up!"

Mr. Jennings said, "My wife gave me some input!"

Ben laughed and said, "I told Wanda that! We really appreciate you coordinating it for us. We still have to purchase some furniture. We would love it if you and your family would come to dinner soon."

Mr. Jennings said, "We would love that! Just let us know."

Wanda said, "We hope to go furniture shopping soon. So hopefully we can set a date next week."

Mr. Jennings asked, "Have you met Mrs. Boatwright?"

Wanda said, "No, we just got in town yesterday. However, we have been praying for our neighbors already."

Mr. Jennings said, "If she is too much for you to handle, just let me know."

Ben said, "I'm sure it will all work out! We plan to be good neighbors, so she should not have much to complain about!"

Mr. Jennings said, "I hope not, but you never know! She can be censorious."

Ben and Wanda left the courthouse, dropped the film off at the drug store, then headed home. Mary was ready for her meeting. She had a list of ten reasons why she needed the car now instead of waiting until May when she graduated. Mr.

Jennings could not refute her reasoning. He released the bank account Grandpa had set aside for her to purchase a car.

Ben, Wanda, David, Dee, and Mary all went to the Chevrolet dealership on Tuesday. Mary was very frugal with her allotted money. She purchased a grey 1979 Monte Carlo with dark grey, fabric interior. That left a good amount of money in her account for future oil changes and scheduled maintenance.

David did not have as many choices. He did find a white cargo van that he liked. It was not as stylish as he wanted, but it served the purpose of transportation and transporting large amounts of food. Dee reminded David that this was not going to be his only vehicle. That after he graduated and opened the café, he would have money to purchase the stylish car he wanted. David agreed. The cargo van was equipped with air conditioning, cruise control, and an FM radio with a cassette player.

The van cost more than David had saved. Ben was able to convince David to let him pay for the van. At the end of the day, Tommy Savor made two more sales to the Davis' family. David and Dee drove off in the new van. Mary was already gone in her new car.

On Thursday, Ben and Wanda drove to Macon to look at property for the new sporting goods store. They found two great locations. One was in the midst of a busy shopping center. The other location was a stand-alone building with great parking. Wanda requested the bylaws for the shopping center. They would make their decision based on the requirements and guidelines listed in the shopping center's bylaws.

During the drive back to Fairville, Ben said, "I've been thinking. Do you think your parents would allow us to pay off the mortgage for their house?"

Wanda said, "Wow! I had not thought of that. I do know, they bought the house when I was around six years old. So, you're right, they're probably still paying on it."

Ben said, "You mentioned last year that your mom went back to work."

Wanda said, "Yes, I don't think it was because of money. She had breast cancer a few years ago and she had to stop working. However, after she recuperated from the surgery and chemotherapy, she wanted to go back to work."

Ben said, "Let's ask them if we can pay off the mortgage."

Wanda asked, "When do you want to ask them?"

Ben said, "I don't feel we should wait. Let's go to Warner Robins this weekend."

Wanda said, "I think it's a great idea. We have to be able to justify where we are getting the money from."

Ben said, "Well, the event center and store have all done well. We can say something about sharing the profits with our family."

Wanda said, "If I were them, I would believe that!"

Ben laughed.

Ben and Wanda made plans to drive over to Warner Robins on Saturday morning. It was Friday afternoon, they went for a run in the neighborhood, and were walking home. Ben saw a small dog standing in road.

Wanda said, "I'm sure that dog belongs to someone in the neighborhood. I don't think it's a stray."

Ben said, "I'll check the collar for information."

As Ben was picking up the six-pound dog, he heard someone screaming at the top of their voice.

The lady demanded, "Put my dog down! That dog belongs to me. Don't steal my dog!"

Ben turned around and a lady was running toward him.

Ben said calmly, “I was not trying to steal your dog. I was just checking the collar for owner information.”

The lady said vociferously, “I’m Agnes Boatwright. This is my dog and I don’t appreciate you touching it. Keep your hands off my dog!”

Ben put the dog down then said, “My name is Ben Davis. This is my wife, Wanda. We live right across the street.”

With disdain Agnes Boatwright reviled, “Oh! I should have known. You’re the person Mr. Cason would always talk about!”

Ben smiled.

Agnes Boatwright said, “I don’t appreciate you touching my dog. Please keep your hands off and do not ever speak to me again in the future.”

Wanda said, “Ma’am, we were just trying to help!”

With her hand on her hip, Agnes Boatwright asked vehemently, “Do I look like I need your help?”

Agnes Boatwright’s hubris was evident. She picked up her dog and walked swiftly into her yard.

Ben asked, “What just happened?”

Shocked Wanda said, “We met Mrs. Agnes Boatwright and she does not like us!”

2

A RAM IN THE BUSH

The two-hour drive to Warner Robins was beautiful. It was a hot summer day in Georgia no rain in the forecast. Ben and Wanda talked and laughed the entire trip. They really enjoyed being together.

Wanda said, "Dad wants to go fishing!"

Ben said, "That's fine. I enjoy fishing with him."

Wanda said, "While you're fishing, I think Momma and I will go shopping for furniture. Unless you want to go with me!"

Ben exclaimed, "Oh no! Please go with Momma. I'm fine. If you see anything you like, buy it!"

Wanda laughed!

Ben said, "I remembered something that I did not tell you about our finances!"

Wanda asked, "What else can there be? Whatever you say, can't add to my current state of shock."

Ben said, "Good! Remember, I told you about the last letter Grandpa left for me."

Wanda said, "Yes, you never told me what it said."

Ben said, "He told me how much he loved me and how

proud of me he was. He told me to keep my heart open because God was sending me a woman that would love me more than I could imagine."

Wanda smiled and said, "He was right!"

Ben smiled and said, "He also told me the story about the display case!"

Wanda said, "I noticed that it was not in the store."

Ben said, "I'll let you read the letter. Grandpa said that the display case was given to him by his father."

Wanda said, "Yes!"

Ben said, "Well, his father's best friend was a black man who was a blacksmith. His name was John T. Baldwin. They went hunting one day and shot a wild boar. They returned to Grandpa's father's land to dig a hole to roast the wild boar. In the hole they found a confederate army bag full of gold."

Wanda exclaimed, "What!"

Ben said, "Yes. John T. melted the gold down and made a few things. He made several candlestick holders, and a few other things. He also made the display case that Grandpa had."

Wanda exclaimed, "That display case is made of pure gold!"

Ben said, "Yes, it is! There were also a few candlestick holders in Grandpa's house."

Wanda asked, "What did you do with them?"

Ben said, "I put them in a safe deposit drawer in the bank!"

Wanda said, "Good, I'm glad we can't tell anyone. This story gets harder and harder to believe."

Ben said, "I know! Neither Mr. Jennings nor Mr. Stevens know about the display case."

Wanda said, "Wow!"

Ben said, "Grandpa also gave me a point of contact in Atlanta. That man will sell gold for us if we ever need money. Grandpa said that he expects me to continue to increase the portfolio, but if there is ever a time that we need additional money. The display case is our safety net."

Wanda said, "I'm in shock! I did not think anything else would shock me."

Ben laughed.

Wanda said, "Do you miss burnishing the display case?"

Ben smiled and said, "I do miss it. It took a lot of time, but it was somewhat relaxing."

Wanda said, "I can't believe that Grandpa thought of everything!"

Ben said, "Yes, he did!"

Wanda said, "He loved you very much!"

Ben said, "I know. I love him too!"

Wanda said, "We can't let him down. We have to increase this portfolio to the best of our ability. We don't ever want to use that safety net!"

Ben said, "I agree!"

Wanda said, "We would be bad businessmen if we lost forty-five million dollars."

Ben said, "I can't imagine. We have been trained for this and prepared by God to take our portfolio to not only the next level, but beyond."

Wanda laughed and said, "I totally agree."

Ben asked, "Have you thought about how we are going to ask your parents about the mortgage?"

Wanda said, "No, I was hoping you had some ideas!"

Ben laughed and said, "Well, I was thinking that we just start the conversation with the truth. Talk about how well the businesses are doing and that we want to bless our family."

Laughing Wanda said, "You know! That's simple but it sounds good!"

As Ben parked the car, he leaned over and kissed his wife.

After he finished, Wanda pulled him back and said, "I love you Ben Davis!"

Ben said, "I love you more!"

As they were getting out of the car, Wanda's mom walked out of the house.

With outstretched arms, Momma said, "Ben, Wanda, I'm so glad to see you!"

Ben hugged his mother in law and said, "We are glad to see you too!"

Wanda said, "Momma, you seem stressed! Is everything OK?"

Momma said, "Nothing we can't handle!"

Wanda said, "So that means there is something wrong!"

Momma said, "We're fine, come on in!"

Ben looked at Wanda. Wanda lifted her shoulders in confusion. As they walked into the house, Wanda saw her father at the table. He stuffed some envelopes in a large manila envelope.

Walking fast toward her dad Wanda said, "Dad, I'm so happy to see you!"

Dad said, "Hello baby girl. I'm always happy to see you!"

Ben asked, "Do you have fishing plans for us this weekend?"

Dad said, "Of course I do!"

Ben said, "Before we start having fun, Wanda and I have something that we want to discuss with you!"

Momma asked, "Wanda! Are you pregnant already?"

Wanda exclaimed, "No, Momma!"

Momma said, "Well, it would not be a bad thing!"

Ben said, "We look forward to having children soon, but not right now!"

Everyone sat down at the table.

Ben said, "What we have to say is not bad news. It's good news!"

Dad said, "That's good to hear. We could use some good news right now!"

Looking at her parents Wanda said, "I know something is going on, but you can tell us later."

Ben said, "It has almost been a year since we opened the event center and it's doing very well. It has been five months since we opened the sporting goods store."

Momma said, "That's wonderful."

Ben said, "We're working on opening another sporting goods store in Macon, hopefully next year."

Dad exclaimed, "That is good news!"

Ben adjusted himself in his seat then took a deep breath.

Ben said, "We have done so well that we would like to bless our family. We want to pay off your mortgage!"

Wanda said, "I know this is a big gift, but we want to do it!"

Momma stood up and asked, "Why would you want to do that?"

Ben said, "It's simple. We want to bless our family with some of our profits."

Dad said, "You don't even know how much our mortgage is!"

Ben said, "Well sir, if it's too much for us to pay off, we can certainly make a big dent in it!"

Everyone laughed.

Momma asked, "Wanda! Did Robert say anything to you?"

Wanda asked, "About what? What could he have said to me?"

Dad said, "We got a second mortgage on the house a few years ago to cover some of the medical expenses that the insurance would not pay when your mother was ill."

Wanda said, "I didn't know that!"

Momma said, "Your dad and I were just discussing how we

were going to pay these bills. Your dad has been laid off of his job at the Air Force Base."

Dad said, "As you know I work for a contractor. They were not renewed to continue working on the base. For the last twenty years, the contractor I work for has always received the contract. However, this year they did not. Of course, they expect the new contractor to hire the existing people, but there are no promises. Rumor has it that the new contractor will be making cutbacks."

Wanda said, "Well, this gift of love could not come at a better time."

With tears running down her face Momma said, "You're right. It's a gift of love!"

Dad said, "Ben, I still feel funny about letting you do this. We're not talking about just the mortgage on the house. We're talking about the second mortgage too."

Ben smiled and said, "I do believe that God laid it on my heart for us to do this. So, it does not matter if it is one mortgage or two. We will take care of them both for you."

Wanda said lovingly, "Dad, this is not a loan. It's a gift!"

Dad smiled and said, "It's a mighty big gift!"

Ben said, "We serve a mighty big God!"

Everyone said, "Amen!"

Wanda said, "I'm so glad that we can do this for you."

Ben asked, "Do you need anything else?"

Dad said, "Oh no, if you could take care of this. We will be fine."

Ben said, "Well, consider it taken care of!"

Dad said, "Well, with that issue not stressing me out, I can enjoy some fishing with my son!"

Ben stood up and said, "I was reading a magazine article and it suggested using strips of squid as bait."

Dad exclaimed, “I tried that before, it didn’t work. However, I’m willing to try it again!”

Wanda waved and said, “You all have a good time!”

Momma said, “Wanda, we can’t thank you enough!”

Wanda smiled and said, “No thanks is needed. I need some furniture for the house, you feel like going shopping!”

Momma laughed and said, “I always feel like shopping!”

Ben and Dad caught more fish than normal using squid as bait. Wanda and her mother were able to find living room and guest room furniture. Wanda wanted to leave the other two bedrooms empty for future children. Ben and Wanda had a great time. They decided to leave on Monday morning. They planned to stop by the realtor’s office in Macon to discuss the property and stop by the university, so Ben could register for upcoming graduate classes.

They agreed to purchase the stand-alone property. Even though they had not reviewed the bylaws of the shopping center. Wanda felt that in the future having to deal with other store owners or a shopping center owner could possibly cause a problem. Ben agreed.

As they were walking into the College of Business building on the Middle Georgia State University campus, they looked around to see if anything had changed.

Ben said, “It still looks the same.”

Wanda laughed.

Dean Smith was coming out of his office.

Ben said, “Good morning sir!”

Dean Smith exclaimed, “How is my favorite couple doing?”

Wanda replied, “We are great!”

Dean Smith asked, “Did you enjoy the honeymoon?”

Ben smiled and said, “Yes we did!”

Dean Smith said, “Well, it’s time for classes again!”

Ben said, "I know. I'm here to register. I know I missed regular registration because we were in Atlanta."

Dean Smith said, "No problem! I will take care of you! Anything for you Ben!"

Ben laughed!

Dean Smith said, "Come on into my office!"

Ben and Wanda took a seat.

Dean Smith asked, "What do you want to take this semester?"

Ben said, "I need to go ahead and finish this degree. So, I want to take three courses this semester and in the spring."

Dean Smith said, "That will require you to drive up at least two days a week!"

Ben said, "I know, but I need to finish!"

Wanda said, "We are opening a new sporting goods store here in Macon. Ben wants to finish his degree as soon as possible."

Dean Smith said, "I think I have an idea. We have a few courses that are called 'independent study.' Those courses require the student to take assignments and finish them on their own."

Ben exclaimed, "That sounds great!"

Dean Smith said, "I will declare a graduate class for you this semester and next semester. Those will be independent study. We can call those classes 'Entrepreneurial Study.' I will come up with a curriculum based on starting a business. What do you think about that!"

Wanda said, "It's a great idea."

Ben asked, "So, I would not have to go to class weekly?"

Dean Smith said, "No, I would meet with you once a month to give you assignments for the next month."

Ben said, "That would be great. I could still take two classes on one day a week and that would free me up to work on the new store."

Dean Smith said, "I like it too. We tried this once before, but the student was not dedicated enough to make it work."

Ben said, "Well, you don't have to worry about me."

Dean Smith said, "I know!"

Wanda said, "That's great! Thank you so much Dean Smith!"

Looking at Wanda, Dean Smith said, "So you decided not to get your master's degree!"

Wanda smiled and said, "Yes, sir! We will have the knowledge in the house, so I am good. Anyway, opening the new store is a big project. I like it better than sitting in class!"

Dean Smith said, "Our goal is to train students to do exactly what you and Ben are doing. I could not be prouder."

Ben said, "Thank you sir!"

Dean Smith said, "I really enjoyed the wedding. Thank you for the invite."

Wanda said, "We're so glad that you could come. Unfortunately, we have not had time to go through our wedding gifts. We plan to open them this week."

Dean Smith said, "No problem. I'm very happy for you both. You make a great couple."

Ben said, "Thank you sir!"

Dean Smith said, "Let me work on this for a couple of days, I will give you a call. Then we can register you for class."

Ben and Wanda stood up.

Extending his hand, Ben said, "Thank you again sir!"

When they left the building, Wanda said, "It pays to be one of the dean's favorites."

Ben laughed and said, "Yes, it does!"

The rest of the year flew by. Uncle Robert hired a new

assistant manager. He was able to promote from within and was advertising for a new cashier. Joshua was thinking about applying to college. Mary was busy with all of her activities. David returned to Atlanta. Ben and Wanda closed on the property and started renovating the building in Macon. The grand opening was scheduled for next year June 1980.

Ben suggested that the family have Thanksgiving at the condo in Atlanta. Uncle Robert proposed to Charlene in late September. They planned to get married in a private ceremony for family only at the church on December 15, 1979. There would be a reception in the small room at the celebration center after. David would cater.

The event center continued to do well. Mom had reservations booked through March 1980. Some people traveled an hour to have their events there. There would be family reunions, baby showers, birthday parties, weddings, funeral repasses, and class reunions. Mom was very busy. She kept Mary, Dee, Pam, and her sisters very busy as servers. They were making good money.

Ben worked hard on his graduate classes. Even though he did not have to attend class for the third course, he was constantly writing essays and research papers. Mary continued to thrive during her senior year. She received offers for full scholarships from twelve colleges. She decided to accept the offer from the University of Georgia in Athens, Georgia. She even received several calls from the hospital asking her to come interpret.

David finalized the paperwork for the company to bottle his spaghetti sauce. They proposed to make it available only in the southeast region of the United States. If it did well, they would open distribution to other regions. Bottles of *David's Awesome Spaghetti Sauce* would be on the shelves by February 1, 1980. David was very happy. Culinary school was going well, he continued to excel. He made contacts that would be beneficial in the future.

In January 1980, Mary was not feeling well. Mom took her to the doctor. She needed to have her tonsils taken out. Although it was a simple operation, Mary was not happy. It was a cold day in January, Ben stopped by the house for a visit.

Mom said, "Mary, people have their tonsils taken out every other day!"

Mary said, "I would like to keep all of the body parts that God gave me!"

Ben said, "Mary, we all would like that. However, sometimes there are complications and we have to have surgery."

Mary said, "Truthfully, I'm not afraid. I just don't want to have surgery."

Mom laughed and said, "I understand that! When you were born I had to have a Caesarean section. I was not happy. When your brothers were born, I delivered them naturally. My pregnancy with you was a little difficult. The closer we got to delivery, it was evident that there was a problem."

Mary said, "I didn't know that!"

Mom said, "Your dad was very worried. Of course, this was in 1962. I did not know anyone who had a C-section before."

Mary asked, "What happened?"

Mom said, "I was very nervous. Your dad was truly afraid. I wanted them to give him some anesthesia."

Everyone laughed.

Mom continued, "My mother prayed over me and told me that God would take care of me."

Ben said, "I barely remember our grandmother."

Mom said, "She died shortly after Mary was born, you were five years old. She was right, God had me. When I woke up from the operation, your father was holding Mary in his arms. The rest is history."

Mary said, "OK, of course I know I have to have the operation!"

Ben said, "I'm just glad it happened while you were home and not away in college. Athens is three hours away."

Mary said, "I had not thought about that! OK, let's schedule the operation!"

Mary's operation went fine. She stayed in the hospital for two nights. She had constant visitors. Mom let her eat as much ice cream as she wanted. It was hard for her to talk for a few days, but she found a way to communicate. She had sheets of paper and colored markers ready to relay her messages.

Mom said, "I had not realized how much Mary talked, until she couldn't."

Everyone laughed.

3

A NEW BEGINNING

The spring of 1980 went by fast. Mary was preparing for graduation. There was only one student that had a higher-grade point average (GPA) than her. Mary's GPA was 97.6 for the last four years. The other student's GPA was 97.7. Mary would give the salutatorian address. She was very happy.

Mom said, "Mary, I'm very proud of you. You have done so well in school. You speak two foreign languages fluently. You served as president or vice president for at least five of your clubs. You're a hard worker and still very humble. You're very impressive."

Mary said, "Thanks Mom. I'm happy with my accomplishments. I'm very excited about giving a speech at the graduation."

Mom asked, "How long can you speak?"

Mary said, "I can speak for four minutes. How am I going to say everything that I need to say in four minutes?"

Mom laughed.

Ben said, "Well, you're going to have to eliminate some of

the things you want to say. The principal will have a stop watch making sure you don't go over time."

Mary sighed heavily.

Mom said, "Well, you don't need to talk about all four years of high school. You just need to say a few things and talk about the future."

Mary said, "The first draft of my speech is eight minutes."

Ben said, "Mary, that means half of what you want to say will be deleted."

Everyone laughed.

Mom asked, "Ben, do you have a date for your graduation yet?"

Ben said, "Yes, it'll be on May tenth at one o'clock."

Mom asked, "Do you want to rent an event room?"

Ben said, "No ma'am, I don't. I'm just really happy to be finished. I'm graduating Suma Cum Laude again."

Mary asked, "That's great! What are we going to do to celebrate?"

Ben said, "There's a restaurant that Wanda and I really like in Macon. I'll make reservations for the family to have dinner there after the graduation."

Mom said, "That would be fine. We have to do something to celebrate. This is a great accomplishment."

Ben said, "I have been so focused on opening the store in Macon."

Mary said, "That's a big accomplishment too. I can't believe you will have two stores. When is the grand opening?"

Ben said, "The grand opening will be Friday, the sixth of June."

Mary asked, "Will you open another one?"

Ben said, "Not any time soon, Wanda and I need a break.

The store in Macon has not been difficult. I think it has been the commuting back and forth that wore us out."

Mom said, "I'm sure that was difficult."

Ben asked, "Mary, what do you want to do to celebrate your graduation?"

Mary said, "I just want something simple here at the house like you and David did."

Mom said, "That would be great. Our family is growing so there will be more traffic."

Mary said, "I know. I like that!"

Mom said, "David will be getting out of school the Friday before your graduation, Ben."

Ben said, "Great. I can't believe he has completed three years already."

Mary said, "His spaghetti sauce is doing great. I saw some on the shelves in our Piggly Wiggly."

Mom said, "That's also a great accomplishment. I'm very proud of all of my children."

Ben and Mary hugged their mother.

On graduation day, all of the family was very proud of Ben. Dinner at the restaurant was delicious. David was so happy to be home. Deep down he was very happy to see Dee too. After the graduation dinner, the family walked through the new sporting goods store in Macon.

Mom said, "This store is much larger than the Fairville store!"

Wanda said, "Yes, it is!"

Mary said, "I like it. I love these colors. They make me want to shop!"

Everyone laughed.

Wanda said, "You're right. Studies have shown that these colors are calming and make shoppers more relaxed so they spend more time in the store. Therefore, they spend more money!"

Uncle Robert said, "That's very interesting!"

Auntie Charlene asked, "What's left to do before you open? It looks ready!"

Ben said, "We're still waiting on some stock, but most of the work is done. We already hired a manager and assistant manager."

Wanda said, "I still need to hire two more cashiers. I'll start training the staff next week."

Ben said, "So, we will be busy up until the opening. That's only four weeks away."

David said, "Ben, this is a beautiful store."

Ben said, "Thanks! We've worked hard."

Dad said, "Wanda, Ben, I'm very proud of you."

Wanda said, "Thanks Dad."

Momma said, "It's very impressive. I don't exercise. but like Mary I want to shop!"

Everyone laughed.

After the tour of the new store, everyone drove home. Mom and Mary rode with Ben and Wanda. Dee and David rode with Uncle Robert and Auntie Charlene. Wanda's parents drove back to Warner Robins.

When Ben and Wanda finally arrived home, they found an ambulance in the neighborhood. Ben parked the car. Their next-door neighbor walked over to let them know what was going on.

The next-door neighbor greeted, "Evening Ben, Wanda!"

Wanda said, "Hi, Mr. Jefferson. What's going on?"

Mr. Jefferson said, "Mrs. Boatwright tripped over her dog, Buttons."

Concerned Ben asked, "Is she OK?"

Mr. Jefferson said, "Yeah, she's fine. She just sprained her ankle. Buttons broke his left, hind leg."

Wanda asked, "How did that happen?"

Mr. Jefferson said, "When Mrs. Boatwright fell, she fell on Buttons."

Ben said, "I'm sorry to hear that."

Mr. Jefferson said, "I can't believe you are so empathetic towards Mrs. Boatwright. She has tried to ostracize you. She has called everyone in the neighborhood and told us that you tried to steal her dog. She also said that you tried to run over Buttons with your car one time."

Shaking his head Ben said, "You know that's not true."

Mr. Jefferson said, "Everyone knows that it's not true."

Wanda said, "We try to keep our distance from Mrs. Boatwright. We've lived here almost a year. I think we have only seen her three times."

Ben said, "She told me not to ever speak to her again in the future."

Mr. Jefferson laughed and said, "That sounds like her. She's not a hypocrite. She meant what she said. She is very angry and lonely. I have lived in the neighborhood about five years. The previous owners warned me about her. I'm white and I have kept my distance too."

Wanda asked, "Do you think we should do anything for her?"

Mr. Jefferson said, "My wife asked the same thing. I told her no!"

Ben said, "Maybe we can send her a basket of fruit and a bag of doggie snacks."

Wanda said, "I like that idea. We don't have to put our name on it."

Mr. Jefferson said flippantly, "You all can do that! I'm not doing anything."

Ben and Wanda went into the house.

Wanda said, "Ben, I'm very proud of you."

Ben hugged his wife and said, "Thanks sweetheart. I'm really glad it's over."

Wanda asked, "You don't want to get your doctorate degree?"

Ben laughed and said, "No, I do not! I'd rather open another store!"

Wanda said, "The family was very impressed with the new store."

Ben said, "I'm glad, we worked hard."

Wanda said, "Now that the store will be open soon. I was thinking, it's time for me to go off of birth control. We have been married for almost a year."

Ben stopped what he was doing and looked at his beautiful wife.

Wanda asked, "What do you think?"

Ben said, "I think it's a great idea. I'm ready!"

Wanda said, "I am too!"

Ben hugged his wife and twirled her around the room.

Wanda said, "I read that it could take up to six months to conceive when you stop taking the pill."

Ben said, "Um! I don't want you to be disappointed when it doesn't happen immediately."

Wanda said, "I would be disappointed. However, I understand, so I'll be OK!"

Ben said, "I'm excited."

Wanda said, "I am too. You feel like trying to conceive tonight."

Ben smiled and asked, "Have I ever told you that I like the way you think?"

Wanda laughed and said, "You said it a few times!"

Ben picked up his wife and carried her to the bedroom.

The next big event was Mary's graduation. It was held on the football field. It was a beautiful night around eighty-five degrees with a slight zephyr. Her graduating class consisted of 136 students. Mary was not nervous at all. She was prepared. She spoke very eloquently and intelligently. She used her lexicon effectively. Her speech was very enjoyable. She spoke about the years of growth, preparation, and dreams that all students have. She challenged her classmates to make a difference in whatever profession they chose. She also challenged parents to continue supporting their children. You never know if you are raising the next President of the United States, the next CEO of a company, or the next teacher. She spoke for exactly four minutes.

Everyone was very proud of Mary. She had become a very accomplished young lady. Her future was bright and she was ready.

The next three weeks flew by. Ben and Wanda hired and trained all of the employees. Wanda hired a photographer and set up a face painting station for the children for the grand opening. Free hotdogs and punch would be available from eleven o'clock in the morning to one o'clock in the afternoon. There was a table out front for customers to sign up for the mailing list to receive coupons in the future. Ben requested police presence during the first week. There was also a table in the front of the store for customers to sign up for door prizes. Drawings would be held three different times throughout the day.

Early on Friday, June sixth, Ben and Wanda gathered the

team together in the break room. Ben prayed. Wanda rallied the team with a chant. The new manager was very excited, he spoke words of encouragement to the team. Everyone was ready. There was a line of customers waiting at the door. The parking lot was full. At nine o'clock, Wanda opened the door and the store quickly filled up.

Ben tried to get to the front of the store, but was delayed by all of the traffic. It was a wonderful day. All of the family stopped by the store. David and Dee brought soup, sandwiches, and desserts for all of the team members. The photographer took a great picture of Ben and Wanda in front of the store.

One of the local radio stations set up out front and broadcasted on location. The local television news stopped by to get a story. The stock room was larger than the one at the original store, Ben figured there would be enough stock to last two weeks.

Ben reserved a hotel room, so he and Wanda would not have to drive the hour and half back to Fairville and come back on Saturday morning. At the end of the first day, everyone was exhausted. Ben and Wanda retreated to their hotel room to rest.

Ben said, "Wanda, I can't believe how great today went."

Wanda said, "I'm still excited. I love grand openings at our stores."

Ben said, "We learned a lot from opening the first store. I think this grand opening was much smoother."

Wanda said, "I jotted down a few lessons learned, but overall everything went great."

Ben said, "I know you did not get a chance to eat. So, I ordered some room service for us."

Wanda asked, "What am I going to do with you? You're so thoughtful!"

Ben said, "I was hoping you would keep me!"

Wanda laughed and said, "There's no way that I'm letting you go!"

Ben said, "Our one-year anniversary is coming up soon. Do you want to go back to the condo?"

Wanda said, "I would love that!"

Ben said, "Hopefully everything will be running smoothly at the new store. I was thinking we could stay two weeks!"

Wanda said, "I really like that idea!"

There was a knock at the door. Wanda opened the door to let the room service attendant in. Her olfactory senses were activated. The smell of the food reminded her of how hungry she was. During dinner, they watched the news to see the footage from the store. They were very pleased with the media reports. They prayed and thanked God for the opportunity. They asked for the wisdom needed to lead their teams and serve the community.

The next day was just as busy as the first day. All of the customers were very pleased with the merchandise and prices. Wanda surveyed many of the customers asking for suggestions for improvements. Many people could not think of anything; however, a few gave some legitimate suggestions.

Ben and Wanda planned to spend Saturday night at the hotel again. The store was closed on Sunday, so they drove back home. When they arrived home, they found Buttons lying in their driveway.

Ben looked at Wanda and asked, "What do we do?"

Wanda shook her head and laughed.

Ben got out of the car, picked up the six-pound dog, and put him in Mrs. Boatwright's driveway. As they were getting out of the car, they saw Mrs. Boatwright pick up her dog and walk back toward her house. They rested most of the day. David and Dee stopped by.

Ben asked, "Would you like to stay for dinner?"

Dee said, "No, we already have plans."

David said, "I have some ideas! I want your opinion."

Everyone sat in the living room.

Wanda asked, "What's up?"

David said, "I still have one year left before graduation. I've started to make money from my spaghetti sauce."

Ben said, "That's great!"

David said, "As you know Grandpa left me the old city café. The building next to the café is for sale."

Wanda asked, "Are you thinking about purchasing it?"

David said, "Yes, the old city café is not that big. If I purchased the building next door, I could have a larger kitchen and more storage area."

Ben said, "That's a great idea."

Dee said, "He has enough money to purchase the building."

Wanda said, "That's great. Is there a problem?"

David said, "No real problem. If I purchase the building, it will take all of my savings. I want to ask Mr. Jennings to give me my trust fund early."

Ben said, "That's a great idea. Grandpa said that there would be enough money in it for you to renovate the city café and have some left over."

David asked, "I was wondering if you knew how much was in the trust fund?"

Shaking his head Ben said, "I don't know!"

Wanda said, "Mary was able to convince Mr. Jennings to give her the car money early. I'm sure he would release your trust fund early too."

Ben said, "If for some reason he can't legally release your trust fund until you graduate, we would let you have the money."

Wanda said, "Of course!"

David said, "It would only be a loan. I graduate in May!"

Ben said, "Not a problem."

David said, "I plan to go talk to Mr. Jennings tomorrow. I just wanted to talk to you first."

Ben said, "David, I'm very proud of you."

David hugged his brother and Wanda.

Wanda asked, "When you purchase the building next door, will you start renovation before you graduate?"

David said, "Dee suggests that I start renovations in January. I graduate in May so, hopefully the renovations will be almost done when I graduate."

Ben said, "That's a great plan!"

Wanda said, "Thanks for providing lunch for the team on Friday. They really enjoyed it."

David said, "I'm glad. Dee helped me."

Ben smiled and said, "It was very thoughtful of you. I really want to pay you."

David said, "No, we wanted to do it."

Wanda said, "Thank you for being so kind and supportive."

Dee said, "We hate to leave, but we're going to the movies."

Ben said, "Great, what's playing?"

David said, "Raiders of the Lost Ark with Harrison Ford."

Wanda exclaimed, "I want to see that!"

Ben said, "Let us know how it is!"

Dee asked, "Do you want to go bowling this week?"

Wanda said, "I would love that. Now that the store is open, maybe we can have some fun."

Ben said, "OK, how about Tuesday?"

David said, "Tuesday would be great. We have to go. We'll see you tomorrow."

Mr. Jennings was able to release part of David's trust fund

early. His trust fund was divided into two parts. The first portion was payable upon graduation from college. He would not be able to receive the second portion until he turned twenty-five years old.

Mr. Jennings had always been impressed with David. However, he was extremely impressed with David's plan to purchase and renovate the building next door to create his own café. Timothy Stevens negotiated a better deal for David to purchase the building. Grandpa was very generous. The first part of the trust fund contained $250,000. It was more than enough to purchase the building for $35,000 and renovate both, with a lot left over.

Mary scheduled a date to go visit the University of Georgia campus in June. All of the family went with her. Ben rented a van, so everyone could ride in one vehicle. Athens was three hours away. It was a very scenic drive. When they arrived at the visitor center, the family was in awe. The campus was so big and beautiful. The tour guide introduced himself and explained that the campus is too large to walk.

Ben asked, "Are you allowed to ride in the van with us?"

Barry, the tour guide, said, "Yes, I am."

Mary exclaimed, "OK, then let's go!"

The tour took about two hours and the family still had not seen everything. They toured the student union, library, and the freshman dorm. There were three cafeterias located on different sides of the campus. They drove past the huge football field, Stanford Stadium. It held approximately 92,000 fans. They toured the athletic center and infirmary.

Mary decided to major in Cultural Studies. She wanted to work in international relations. The family toured the Cultural Studies building. It was a very tall building with ten floors. The student population for the University of Georgia was approximately 26,000. The town of Fairville only had a population of 9,000 people.

After the official tour, Mary took the family to the areas she had been during her summer camp on campus. She was very excited. The family had dinner in Athens. Everyone talked about what they had seen.

Dee said, "Mary, that is such a large campus."

Mary said, "I know. When I was here for the summer, it was overwhelming."

Wanda said, "I have never seen anything like it."

Mom said, "I'm still in shock. Mary, are you sure you want to attend a school this big?"

Mary said, "I am positive. I like it!"

Ben said, "Well, we have always known that you were a big fish. Fairville was too small for you."

Everyone laughed.

David said, "The campus reminds me of Atlanta. Everywhere you look, there is something new."

Mary said, "I'm not afraid, I'm excited."

Wanda said, "Watch out University of Georgia, Mary Davis is on her way!"

Everyone laughed.

The rest of the summer flew by. On August sixteenth, Mary packed her car and drove back to Athens. Everyone cried.

Mom said, "The house is going to be so empty and quiet. Mary is gone. David will be leaving in a couple of days."

Ben said, "I know. Mom if you want to, you can move in with us."

Mom said firmly, "I do not want to move in with you and Wanda. However, thanks for the invitation."

Wanda said, "Well, let's make a standing dinner date. We'll have dinner with you at least one day of every week."

Mom said, "I like that. Of course, I'll get over this sadness. This is what I raised my children for. I want them to leave the nest. The event center has been keeping me busy. I have friends that I've been neglecting. I'll be fine."

David said, "I'll be home in May of next year. I plan to make more visits home starting in January. That's when I'll start renovating the café."

Mom said, "You're right. I will be fine."

Mary called to say that she had made it to Athens safely. A few days later, David left. Everyone was sad again. Dee could not stop crying. She and David had gotten really close over the summer. David was not calling her his girlfriend. He said they were just good friends.

4

CELEBRATING FAMILY MILESTONES

Mary settled into her dorm room, she knew not to pack too much. She tried to vary her clothing. She packed dresses, pants, and shorts. However, she still felt that she brought too much. She left the door ajar for her new roommate. As Mary was busying herself with unpacking, she heard a loud voice in the hallway. As she turned around a beautiful white girl with brunette hair was walking through the door.

Mary said, "Hi, I'm Mary Davis."

The girl said, "Hi, my name is Eva Thompson. I am from North Carolina. I am majoring in Cultural Studies. I have one older brother. My father died when I was young. My mother is a nurse at our local hospital. I drove down all by myself. I speak two foreign languages and I love pizza."

Mary smiled and said, "Wow! You just gave me your biography."

Eva said, "I am sorry. Some people say I am loquacious. I really don't think so. I just try to tell people what I think they need to know."

Mary laughed and said, "I totally understand. I have gotten

better over the years, I try to make sure that what I say is important. I can talk a lot too!"

Eva said, "Well, I am glad to meet you Mary!"

Mary said, "Did you get a chance to visit the campus during the summer?"

Eva said, "Yes, I did. My mom and I drove down. It's a five-and-a-half-hour drive, but I love to drive. When we first drove down, we went through Charlotte. When we drove back, we drove through Durham. I like the Charlotte way best."

Mary said, "I'm from a small town called Fairville, it's only three hours away."

Eva said, "I see that you have set up on the right side of the room. I'm glad, I really wanted the left. However, I was willing to sacrifice if you wanted the left."

Mary said, "I'm glad it worked out!"

Eva said, "I'm so excited to be here. I just can't stop talking!"

Mary laughed and said, "I know how you feel. I'm also a Cultural Studies major. What two languages do you speak?"

Eva said, "I speak Spanish fluently. I also speak French, but I need to practice more."

Mary said, "Great! I speak Spanish and French fluently. We can practice together."

Eva said, "I can't believe this. I prayed that I would have a lot in common with my roommate. I didn't want a Hedonist."

Mary laughed and said, "I'm glad to hear that you're a Christian too."

Eva said, "Yes, I am. I was baptized when I was eleven years, I have worked in the church all of my life. I was brought up going to Sunday School and Vacation Bible School during the summer. My family went to church every Sunday. Was that too much information?"

Mary laughed and said, "I didn't think so, but other people may think so!"

Eva laughed.

Mary helped Eva unpack her car. Eva brought a lot of things. She brought her television, radio, a trunk filled with clothing, and three large suitcases. After the dorm room was set up, they checked in to all of their required locations. They got lost at least four times on that Saturday. They picked up their class schedule. They were surprised that they had three of their five courses together.

Mary said, "My brother was able to take a test to skip some courses. I don't want to do that."

Eva said, "I don't either."

Mary asked, "Are you on scholarship?"

Eva said, "No, I was not able to qualify. Are you?"

Mary said, "Yes, I'm grateful."

Eva said, "That's great. When my dad passed away, my mom set aside some of the insurance money for me to go to college."

Mary said, "That's great that you don't have to worry about it."

Eva said, "I know. I also worked during the summers, so I have saved some money."

Mary said, "I worked too! You're right, we're a lot alike!"

Eva laughed.

Over the next few days Mary and Eva became great friends. Mary was pleased with all of her instructors. She was scheduled for three classes on Monday, Wednesday, and Friday. The first class was at 8:00 am. On Tuesday and Thursday, she had two classes. The first class was not until 9:30 am.

There were so many clubs to join. Mary did not want to decide too quickly. She finally narrowed it down to two that she was really interested in. Within the College of Cultural Studies, there was a club called Foreign Exchange. This club would interact with foreign students enrolled on campus. She also was interested in becoming a hostess for various events on campus. It took her a while but she finally found that organization. She was on her way to making her mark at the University of Georgia. Mary called home every Sunday evening to talk to Mom, Ben, and Wanda. She wrote David letters. She did not plan to go back home until Thanksgiving.

Her weekends were busy with hosting events and helping international students find their way around campus. She excelled in her courses. She was very happy. Mary was not eligible for as much federal grant money as Ben and David received. Mom was now making substantially more money working at the event center than she did working at the textile factory. Ben made sure Mary had more than enough money in her bank account for anything she wanted to do.

The Macon sporting goods store was doing well. Ben and Wanda felt good about their employees. They felt comfortable only making a trip to check on the store once, sometimes twice a week.

They would fill in for the manager at either store when needed. They realized that they needed an office. They set up one of the empty bedrooms as a home office. That worked out well.

Months passed, Wanda had not conceived. She was concerned. Ben and Wanda ran at least four days a week in the neighborhood. One morning after going for a run, Ben could see that Wanda was stressed.

Ben asked, "Sweetheart, what's wrong?"

Wanda said, "Nothing! What makes you think something is wrong?"

Ben smiled and said, "You know, I know when something is wrong with you!"

Wanda laughed and said, "I have been trying hard not to show it."

Ben said, "I noticed that too!"

Wanda smiled and said, "Suppose something is wrong with me and I can't have children."

Ben said, "I know it has been a few months. I don't think anything is wrong with you."

Wanda said, "My mom did not get pregnant with me until she was thirty-two years old. They had been married for five years."

Ben asked, "Was there anything wrong?"

Wanda said, "She never said there was!"

Ben said, "We trust God. When the time is right, he will give us a child."

Wanda said, "I just don't want to wait and something is wrong. I would have wasted time, when I could have been correcting a problem."

Ben pulled his wife close and said, "Let's say that there is something wrong with either you or me, we could adopt!"

Wanda said, "That's true!"

Ben said, "I'm sure the doctors aren't going to do any tests on either of us, until at least six months after we stopped birth control."

Wanda said, "I asked. We have to be off of birth control for at least a year to start any tests."

Ben said, "OK, it has only been what three months. Let's just relax and continue to enjoy the process."

Wanda smiled and said, "Well, I hope that even after I conceive we will enjoy the process."

Ben pulled her close and laughed.

David and Mary returned home for Thanksgiving week. Mom reserved the small room at the celebration center for dinner. David wanted to cook. He and Dee cooked everything. Everyone gathered together for dinner.

Mom said, "I'm so glad that everyone could be here today. I'm so thankful to have all of my children in one city. I'm also happy to share this holiday with you."

Uncle Robert stood up and said, "I'm so thankful to be here with my wife. Charlene and I have been married now for eleven months. I have never been happier. Dee will be graduating from high school this year. I have a wonderful job that I love. Sometimes I feel guilty that I'm so blessed."

Everyone laughed.

Auntie Charlene stood up and said, "All of you know how thankful I am to be a part of this family. For years, I kept dropping hints to Robert to ask me out. He never did."

Everyone laughed.

Auntie Charlene continued, "It was worth the wait. I have never been so happy. God has blessed me with a husband that I adore. It seems he adores me just as much. I now have a daughter whom I love dearly. I can't stop smiling."

Dad stood up and said, "Denise and I are doing great. After being laid off for six months, the new contractor hired me back. Part of me had gotten use to staying home. I love my job and I thank God every day for my family."

Mary stood up and said, "I'm so thankful for my university. I love it. It seems that everywhere I go, someone knows my name."

Everyone laughed.

Mary continued, "I'm doing well in all of my classes. I really like my roommate. We're good friends. I think I finally met someone that talks more than me."

Everyone laughed.

David stood up and said, "I'm very thankful that I'm in my last year of culinary school. Everyone is invited to the graduation in May. I'm excited. I'll start renovation on the old city café in January. So hopefully next summer I will have a café."

Mary asked, "Have you decided on a name?"

David said, "Yes! Dee suggested David's Soups, Sandwiches, and Desserts! It's simple, but I like it."

Everyone agreed.

Dee stood up and said, "I'm thankful that I'll be graduating from high school this year. I plan to attend Middle Georgia State University in Macon. My mom and dad will be happy to have the house to themselves."

Auntie Charlene said lovingly, "That's not true!"

Uncle Robert said, "Yes, it is!"

Everyone laughed.

Dee continued, "So our family will have two graduations next year. David's will be in early May and mine will be in the middle of May."

Ben and Wanda both stood up.

Ben said, "God has blessed our new store. It's doing wonderful. We're already turning a profit. The sales at the Fairville store are continuing to set new sale trends each month. Uncle Robert is doing a great job. Mom manages the event center like she was born to do it. God has blessed us. Wanda and I have now been married about seventeen months. I can't thank God enough."

Wanda said, "My cup runneth over. As you know, Ben and I have been trying to conceive. Well, God has blessed. We're pregnant!"

Everyone jumped up!

Mom said, "Oh my goodness. That's wonderful!"

Momma said, "I'm so happy for you! I can't wait to go shopping!"

Dad said, "Congratulations. I'm going to be a grandpa! I'm very happy!"

Mary said, "That's wonderful. Do you want to know what the sex is before the baby is born?"

Ben said, "We don't. We want to wait for the delivery."

David said, "I'm so happy for you! I think when I have a child, I want to be surprised too!"

Dee said, "That sounds nice!"

Everyone laughed.

Uncle Robert said, "Congratulations! Wow, this family is starting to grow!"

Everyone enjoyed the delicious dinner. David prepared the traditional, southern Thanksgiving dinner. He cooked collard greens, peas, yams, cornbread dressing, turkey, ham, macaroni & cheese, and fresh baked rolls. He made cakes and pies for dessert. There was so much food, everyone took home containers.

At the beginning of 1981 David started the renovation of his two buildings. He had already drawn up the plans. He hired Frank McCants as the contractor. Dee would serve as his point of contact while he was away in Atlanta. The spring went by fast. Wanda's pregnancy was going well. Wanda suffered from very little morning sickness. She and Ben continued to run at least three times a week. They both were in great shape. They worked hard to be strong and limber.

Mary continued to excel and make a name for herself at the university. She was not coming home for spring break. She planned to go home with Eva to Raleigh, North Carolina. The renovation of the café slowed down due to weather. There was an atypical snow storm in February. The city was closed down for almost two weeks. When renovation continued, there were problems getting supplies.

The café was not going to be ready in July as David had planned. It probably would not be completed until early August. David was sad, but he was also busy with his spaghetti sauce. He was now making public appearances to promote the product.

David's graduation was scheduled for May 9, 1981. Ben rented a van so that all of the family could ride to Atlanta together. Uncle Robert and Auntie Charlene planned to stay in a hotel. Everyone else would stay at the condo. It would be crowded but that was fine. Mary planned to drive down from Athens.

The graduation started at 10:00 am. It lasted about two hours. There were 750 students in David's class. David graduated with honors, Magna Cum Laude. At the end when all of the graduates were told to put on their *toque blanche*, it was very emotional. Toque blanche is French for white hat. That is what the chef hat is called. Everyone was very proud of David.

David made reservations at a restaurant in Atlanta. The food was delicious. Everyone had a great time. The family stayed in Atlanta until Sunday afternoon. David took Dee sightseeing. Uncle Robert and Auntie Charlene had plans of their own. Wanda's parents had tickets to a Broadway play on Saturday night.

Ben, Wanda, Mom, and Mary toured Underground Atlanta. They shopped until they dropped. They had a wonderful time. Mary had developed into a beautiful young lady. She was turning heads of young men everywhere they went.

Mom said, "Mary, you have not mentioned anything about the men at the university."

Mary said, "There are a lot of them, all different nationalities."

Wanda asked, "Is it too many to choose from?"

Mary said, "I'm not focused on young men right now. I've been so busy."

Ben said, "I'm sure one of those young men has asked you out."

Mary said, "Oh, yes! Many have asked me out. However, I have not said yes to any of them yet."

Wanda said, "Don't rush. The right one will make you want to say yes. He will be worth the wait. Ben was!"

Mary smiled and said, "I'm content. I stay busy. In October, I'll be going to Spain for three weeks."

Mom said, "Spain! Oh, my goodness!"

Ben laughed and said, "That's great. Will Eva be going too?"

Mary said, "Yes, she and I are both very excited."

The next two weeks seemed to fly by. Dee's graduation was scheduled for one o'clock on Saturday. The entire family was assembled in the bleachers of the football field. Dee was graduating Magna Cum Laude. She was very happy. She looked very nice. Everyone noticed how David was smiling.

Joshua and John were also graduating. Joshua planned to go to Middle Georgia State University too. John was going into the Marine Corps. He was scheduled to leave for boot camp on July tenth. All of the team members attended the graduation to support them. Ben and Wanda established full scholarships for all team members that wanted to attend college, despite their age.

After the graduation, everyone met at Uncle Robert's house. Auntie Charlene prepared dinner. David baked a Red Velvet Cake. That was Dee's favorite. Everyone had a great time.

Everyone was happy that Mary and David were home. Mary continued to work at the event center. David catered whenever he could. There were still product meetings in Atlanta, that he had to attend regarding his spaghetti sauce. There were also meetings that he had to attend for the café. Final preparations were being made for the interior of the café. Mom relished in having all of her children together again.

5

HE COVERED ME!

The summer was beautiful in Fairville. Wanda was now six months pregnant. Everything was going fine. The second store in Macon was doing very well. Ben was very happy with his employees and the managers that he hired. Ben and Wanda would make a trip to Macon at least twice a week on different days to ensure all was going well.

It was another beautiful summer day in June, Ben and Wanda planned to work in the Fairville store. Uncle Robert had some appointments. It was about fifteen minutes after one in the afternoon. Wanda was working the cash register, while one of the team members took a break. There were only about ten customers in the store. A white man with a backpack walked into the store. He walked around the store for about ten minutes. He walked up to the cash register. Wanda could see that he was nervous.

Wanda greeted, "Good afternoon, may I help you?"

The man said, "Yes, give me all of the money in the cash register!"

Not wanting to believe what she heard, Wanda said, "I'm sorry. I didn't hear you clearly."

The man said louder, "Give me the money in the cash register."

Wanda said calmly, "No problem. Do you have something you would like for me to put it in?"

Irritated the man said, "Just put it in plastic bag. Hurry up!"

When Wanda leaned down to get a bag, she pressed the silent alarm that was on the side of the cabinet that was beneath the cash register. The man was angry that it was taking her so long.

The man said loudly, "Hurry up or I will shoot you right now."

The man then dropped his bookbag and pulled out a nine-millimeter hand gun.

Wanda said calmly, "Sir, I am working as fast as I can."

While working in the office, Ben saw that the silent alarm had been pressed. This alarm notified the local police department directly. He left the office to check everything out. When he walked into the shopping area, he looked for Wanda. Then Ben saw the man with the gun. He tried to walk quietly, but his long legs were taking steps as long as his six-foot frame could make. At this time the man was clearly waving the gun at Wanda. One lady saw the gun, screamed, and ran to the back of the store. This only made the man more frustrated. When Wanda tried to give him the bag, he dropped the bag of money on the floor.

As he was picking up the bag, he yelled, "This is all the money you have in that cash register!"

Wanda replied, "Yes sir, that's all. We have not been open long."

The man yelled, "You think I'm dumb. I'm not dumb! Open the other cash register!"

As Wanda stepped over to the other cash register, the man pointed the gun and shot into the wall to the right of her. Wanda jumped! At this time, Ben was about three feet from her in front of the cash registers.

Ben asked calmly, "Good afternoon sir, do you need some help?"

The man exclaimed, "No, I don't! I'm about to pop a bullet in her!"

Ben said, "Sir! Please relax and put down your gun."

The man exclaimed, "I have a better idea, why don't I just shoot her! How about that!"

He pointed the gun straight at Wanda. Wanda turned her shoulder and crouched down low to protect the baby. Ben leaped, stretching his body as long as he could.

The man fired two shots! The first shot missed Wanda; the second was headed straight for her. Ben's body intercepted the bullet. The man dropped the gun and ran. As he was running out of the door with the bag of money in his hand, the police caught him and wrestled him to the floor. Wanda stood up and saw Ben's body on the floor.

She screamed, "Ben! Somebody dial 911. Call 911!"

Instantly tears jumped out of her eyes as she cradled Ben's head in her lap.

Struggling to speak Ben asked, "Are you OK?"

Wanda said, "I'm fine. Are you OK?"

Trying to get up Ben said slowly, "Yeah, I'm good."

Wanda saw the blood coming out of his body, she cried, "Ben, you're not OK!"

By this time, a policeman was at her side. He covered Ben with a blanket, then tried to put constant pressure on his wound.

Uncle Robert tried to pulled Wanda away, but she fought

back and screamed, "I'm not going anywhere. God help me! Where is the ambulance?"

Uncle Robert said, "They're on their way. Wanda, let's pray!"

Uncle Robert was able to move her over to the wall as the policemen worked diligently on Ben trying to figure out exactly where the bleeding was coming from. Wanda cried, while Uncle Robert prayed. Uncle Robert heard the sirens and thanked God that the ambulance was in route. Only three minutes passed, but it seemed like an eternity. When the policeman moved, Wanda saw that Ben was reaching for her. His clothes and the floor had blood all over them. Wanda dropped to her knees and took his hand.

Struggling to speak Ben asked, "Are you sure that you're OK?"

Wiping her tears, Wanda said, "Sweetheart, I'm fine. I love you!"

In noticeable pain Ben said, "I love you more!"

The paramedic was not able to stop the bleeding. They transferred Ben to a stretcher, then transported him to the hospital leaving a trail of blood. Uncle Robert drove Wanda to the hospital. Wanda cried and prayed all the way. While in the emergency room waiting for a report, Uncle Robert called the family to tell them what happened. It did not take long for Mom, Mary, Dee, and David to arrive. Uncle Robert gave them the report. Finally, after an hour the doctor entered the waiting room to give the family an update.

The doctor said, "Good afternoon, my name is Dr. Linnville. We have temporarily stopped the bleeding. Mr. Davis is being prepped for surgery. The bullet is currently lodged in his back-deltoid muscle area. We have to get it out!"

Wanda said, "He lost a lot of blood."

Dr. Linnville said, "Yes, he has. We will have to do a transfusion, but we first have to remove the bullet and get him stable."

Mom asked, "Will you be performing the surgery?"

Dr. Linnville said, "Yes, I don't have time to wait for a more experienced surgeon to get here. If we don't stop the bleeding soon, he will bleed out?"

Dee asked, "What does bleed out mean?"

Wiping his tears David whispered, "It means he could bleed to death."

Covering her mouth Dee gasped.

Wiping her tears Mary asked, "Have you ever done this type of surgery before?"

Dr. Linnville replied, "I have done surgeries similar to this. I feel confident."

Uncle Robert asked, "Do you mind if we pray for you?"

Dr. Linnville said, "No, I don't. I would appreciate it."

The family gathered around Dr. Linnville. Uncle Robert prayed for God to guide her in the surgery, to give her the knowledge and skills to accurately remove the bullet, and repair any tendons or muscles that needed to be repaired. He thanked God for the hospital, medical staff, medication, and technology that were available to perform this surgery and save Ben's life.

The nurse interrupted and said, "Dr. Linnville, we are ready."

Mom asked, "How long do you expect the surgery to take?"

Dr. Linnville said, "I really don't know. I expect it to take more than two hours, but I hope that it will not be over four."

With tears rolling down her cheeks and shaking uncontrollably, Wanda said firmly, "I need you to save my husband!"

Dr. Linnville said, "We will do everything that we can. I am confident that we can remove the bullet, then we will be able to stop the bleeding. He may require additional surgeries to correct any muscle repair, but today I am focused on removing the bullet."

Wanda asked, "Can I see him?"

Dr. Linnville said, "No, he is already being prepped. We have to move fast."

Trying to control her tears, Wanda said, "Please, don't wait any longer. Go!"

Dr. Linnville turned around and walked swiftly through the doors.

Mary said, "Wanda, you're covered in blood. You need to change clothes."

Mom asked, "Do you want to go home and take a shower?"

Wanda said quickly and firmly, "No, I can't leave."

Dee suggested, "We can go pick up some clean clothes and toiletries for you."

Mom said, "Great idea. You all go to the house and get her a few things."

Uncle Robert said, "I'm going to run back to the store and close everything up."

Mom said, "That's fine. We'll be here!"

Wanda walked over to the chair, sat down, and cried. Despite her own tears Mom tried to console her.

Wanda asked, "Did Uncle Robert tell you how Ben got shot?"

Mom said, "No, he didn't know the specifics."

Speaking slowing and taking deep breaths Wanda said, "A man tried to rob the store, I was on the cash register. I was able to press the silent alarm when I reached down for the plastic bag. I gave him the money in the drawer. The man was upset that it was not as much money as he thought it would be. He pulled a gun out of his backpack. By that time Ben was standing in front of the cash register."

Mom gasped and said, "Oh my!"

Wiping her tears Wanda expounded, "The man fired a shot to the left of me. I dropped to my knees to cover my stomach. Ben tried to calm the man down. The man then said that he would just pop a bullet into me."

As tears streamed down her face, Mom was in shock.

Wanda continued, "Then he shot above my head, then he lowered his gun to take a better aim at me. I tried to close my eyes, but I couldn't. I saw Ben leap and stretch his body for the bullet to hit him instead of me."

Wiping her tears Mom said, "He loves you very much."

Sobbing Wanda said, "I know. I can't lose him!"

Mom said, "God knows our prayer and he knows how much Ben means to our family. We have to trust that he'll be OK."

Wanda said, "When he was on the floor, he kept asking me, if I was OK."

Mom said, "He wanted to make sure that his sacrifice had not been in vain."

Crying Wanda said, "Mom, I can't lose him."

Wiping her tears Mom said, "Let's focus on the positive. Right now, he's still alive. He's at a hospital that is capable of removing the bullet and stop the bleeding. God brought us to this point, so he will take us through it."

Wanda said, "I believe that."

At that time, Wanda felt the baby kick.

Wanda said, "I just felt the baby kick!"

Mom said, "That's a great sign. Let me try and find you something to drink."

Wanda sat in the chair and continued to pray. She thanked God for her husband, their baby, their family, and everything else she could think of. Mary, David, and Dee returned with a suitcase full of things Wanda and Ben would need. Wanda went into the restroom to clean up. Mom told everyone exactly what had happened.

Mary asked, "Mom, do you think Ben is going to be OK?"

Mom said, "We've all prayed. Let's continue to pray and thank God for his blessings and strength to endure all that's before us. We trust God. We have to believe that he will work this out for our good."

David said, "Yes ma'am. So, what do we do now? Just wait!"

Mom said, "Yes, we continue to pray and wait. Waiting is the hardest part."

Uncle Robert and Auntie Charlene walked into the waiting room. The medical assistant walked over to the family.

The medical assistant said, "I am here to escort you to another waiting room."

Mom asked, "Do you have any information about the surgery?"

The medical assistant apologized, "I'm sorry I don't. The surgery team is aware that you will be waiting in the room that I'm taking you to."

Wanda tried to walk faster.

Mom said, "Wanda, relax. Don't rush!"

Wanda slowed down and tried to walk slower.

Uncle Robert said, "I talked to William and Denise. I told them what happened. They plan to drive over on tomorrow."

Wanda stopped, hugged him, and said, "Thanks Uncle Robert."

Uncle Robert said, "Everyone at the store is praying for

Ben. When I got there the police had already taken their pictures so the floor could be cleaned up. I told the staff that we would be closed tomorrow."

Mary saw Wanda place her hand on her stomach, she asked, "Wanda, are you OK?"

Wanda said, "I thought I was, but I'm starting to cramp really bad!"

Mom said, "Sometimes the excitement can be too much. You may just need to get off your feet."

When they arrived at the waiting room, it was nicer than the one down stairs. David found a recliner and helped Wanda sit down and put her feet up. Mom found a telephone and called Wanda's obstetrician. She explained what was going on. The obstetrician thanked Mom for calling and said that she would stop by the hospital within the hour. Everyone sat around the waiting room trying to stay positive and not worry. The surgery had been going on for two hours.

Mary said, "It's now been two hours, so hopefully it won't be much longer."

Auntie Charlene said, "I'm going to run home and make something for us to eat."

Uncle Robert said, "That would be great. It's going to be a long night, whatever you can do will be great. Sandwiches would be fine."

Auntie Charlene said, "I'll be back as soon as I can."

Wanda laid in the recliner trying to relax.

Dee asked, "Wanda, do you need anything?"

Wanda said, "I'm fine. I have to be. I'm sure God won't let anything happen to our baby."

Dee smiled and said, "I'm sure the baby is fine. You've been through a lot today. You need to rest. You're a strong woman

Wanda and very resilient! I don't think I would be able to handle this!"

Wanda smiled and said, "I know you could. The same God that lives in me, lives in you."

Dee said, "David hasn't asked me to be his girlfriend yet. However, he treats me like I am."

Wanda smiled and said, "It's obvious that he cares a lot about you. I know he's concerned about your age difference. He thinks that once you go to college in a few weeks, you may meet someone else."

Dee said, "No one can change my mind concerning him."

Wanda said, "I know, but that's his concern. So, he doesn't want to tie you down just in case you meet someone else."

Dee asked, "What can I do?"

Wanda said, "Why don't you ask him if he wants to date exclusively. That you're eighteen now!"

Dee said, "OK. If I continue to wait on him, I may be twenty-one, before we're officially a couple."

Wanda laughed!

Time seemed to creep by. Mom found a blanket and covered Wanda.

Wanda said, "Thanks. I feel OK now."

Mom said, "Good. I called your obstetrician earlier. She said that she would stop by and check on you."

Wanda said, "I really am fine, but I guess it won't hurt."

Mom said, "When you see Ben, you want to be able to tell him that you and the baby are fine."

Nodding her head Wanda agreed, "That's true."

Not too long afterwards Dr. Holmes, the obstetrician, walked into the waiting room. She surveyed the room and saw Wanda sitting in the recliner.

Mom said, "Hi doctor!"

Dr. Holmes said, "Good evening. Wanda, how do you feel?"

Wanda said, "I'm fine. Earlier I did have some severe cramps, but I have been lying here for about an hour. I feel much better now."

Dr. Holmes said, "Let me just listen to your heartbeat and the baby's heartbeat."

Putting on her stethoscope, Dr. Holmes listened to both heartbeats. Wanda tried to relax and repose.

She said, "Both of your hearts sound great. Have you noticed any spotting?"

Wanda said, "No, I went to the restroom about fifteen minutes ago."

Dr. Holmes said, "Great. I think it was just the excitement of the day. Is Ben still in surgery?"

Wanda said, "Yes, it's been almost four hours. So, we hope the doctor will come out soon."

Dr. Holmes said firmly, "This is paramount! I need you to get some rest tonight."

Wanda said firmly, "I'm not leaving the hospital tonight. I will be fine. I can't leave Ben."

Dr. Holmes said, "I understand. I will stop by tomorrow morning after I finish my rounds. Please, stay off of your feet as much as you can. The baby needs to calm down and so do you."

Rubbing her belly Wanda said, "I will. We have ten weeks to go. I will keep this baby in."

Dr. Holmes smiled and said, "I'll see you tomorrow after my rounds!"

As Dr. Holmes was leaving the area, Dr. Linnville walked in. The family scurried around her. Mom made Wanda stay seated.

Dr. Linnville walked over to the recliner and said, "Surgery went well. We removed the bullet. We were able to stop the bleeding. That nine-millimeter bullet did a lot of damage. I was able to repair some muscle and tissue damage while I was in there."

Wanda said, "Thank you Lord!"

Mom asked, "So, Ben's no longer in any danger?"

Dr. Linnville said, "He is in no danger. He will require physical therapy, but I believe he will regain full use of his shoulder. It will take a while, but he will be fine."

Uncle Robert asked, "Is he in any pain right now?"

Dr. Linnville said, "Right now he is feeling no pain. When the pain medicine wears off, he will be in pain. We have temporarily installed a morphine pump for him. He will be on pain medicine for a while and he will not be able to use his left arm. He will have to wear a sling, but overall he is fine."

Wanda said, "Thank you doctor. How long will it be before I can see him?"

Dr. Linnville said, "He is in recovery. They are waking him up now, so in about thirty minutes. They will come out here to get you."

Mom asked, "How long will he have to stay in the hospital?"

Dr. Linnville said, "I want him to stay at least two nights. Depending on how things go, hopefully we can release him then."

Mary asked, "What would make you keep him longer?"

Dr. Linnville said, "Well, I have to check his other bodily functions. I am sure he will be fine."

Wanda asked, "What about all of the blood that he lost?"

Dr. Linnville said, "Yes, we had to perform a transfusion. He is fine now!"

Wanda said, "Thank you so much!"

Dr. Linnville asked, "Are you and the baby OK?"

Wanda said, "Yes, we are fine and much better now."

Dr. Linnville said, "OK, everyone can see him soon!"

Charlene returned with sandwiches for everyone. Uncle Robert briefed her on what was happening. Wanda was able to eat half of a sandwich. The nurse entered the waiting room and announced that Ben could have visitors. Wanda went in first. When Wanda walked in, Ben smiled and reached for her.

Wanda hugged her husband tightly and said, "Ben, I was so afraid that I would lose you."

Ben smiled and said, "Remember, God has given us many years together."

Wanda smiled.

Ben asked, "So, you're OK?"

Wanda said, "Ben, I love you!"

Ben said, "I love you too!"

Wanda said, "The baby and I are fine. Dr. Holmes checked us out to make sure."

Ben said, "Good! I can't lose you either!"

Wanda said, "Ben, you sacrificed your life for me!"

Squinting Ben asked, "Why are you surprised? You know how much I love you. I can't lose you!"

With tears rolling down her cheeks Wanda said, "When I think I can't love you any more, you do something to make me fall deeper in love with you."

Wiping her tears with his right-hand, Ben smiled and said, "Good!"

Wanda said, "Everyone is waiting to see you. I will let them come in now."

With his right-hand Ben pulled Wanda close and kissed her.

Wanda said, "I missed you."

Ben said, "I'm glad that I'm back!"

Wanda said, "Me too!"

Wanda told everyone to come in. Everyone surrounded the bed and loved on Ben. He was happy to see his family and they were happy to see him.

Mary said, "Ben, we were so worried about you!"

Mom said, "We're just so thankful that you're going to be alright."

Ben said, "I didn't feel the bullet until I hit the floor."

David asked, "What did it feel like?"

Ben said, "I just felt a lot of pain. At first, I thought it was from hitting the floor. When I tried to get up, I could not move my left arm. I knew then that I was hit. I was just glad it was me and not Wanda."

Wanda smiled and touched his arm.

Ben said, "I don't remember much after that."

Dee said, "I hope I never have to experience anything else like this."

Uncle Robert said, "We all do!"

Mom said, "Ben, the doctors said that you should not be in pain now."

Ben said, "I'm not in pain, but I am hungry!"

Auntie Charlene said, "I made some ham sandwiches."

Ben asked, "May I have one please?"

Auntie Charlene passed him a sandwich. Ben tried not to eat fast.

He said, "This is delicious. I'm so hungry."

Mom said, "Don't eat a lot. I think they want to monitor you for a little while longer."

Finishing up the sandwich, Ben said, "I feel so much better now. Thanks everyone for your prayers."

Passing Ben, a cup of water, Mom said, "As much as we want to stay, we better go, so you can rest."

Everyone hugged Ben carefully, trying not to touch his left side.

As they were walking out of the door Ben asked, "Auntie Charlene, may I have another sandwich?"

Everyone laughed as Auntie Charlene gave Ben another sandwich.

Ben said, "Wanda, I'll see you tomorrow."

Looking back Wanda said, "I'm not going home. I'm just going to the restroom."

Ben said, "Mom, please tell Wanda that she needs to go home and rest."

Mom leaned closer to Ben and said, "She's not leaving and I don't blame her. She almost lost you. If I were her, I would not leave either."

Ben looked at his mom and said, "I know she has been through a lot today. I just want her to rest."

Kissing him on his forehead Mom said, "She will be fine here with you."

Ben smiled.

When Wanda returned from the restroom she said, "Mary, David, and Dee went to the house to pick up some things for us."

Eating his sandwich Ben said, "Good!"

Now that everyone had gone, Wanda stood next to the hospital bed. Ben could see that she was exhausted.

While taking another bite of his sandwich, Ben asked, "Did you eat anything today?"

Wanda said, "I had half of a sandwich earlier."

Ben gave Wanda his sandwich for her to eat.

Wanda smiled and took a bite. It was delicious. Now, that she was not worried about Ben, she realized how hungry she was.

Ben said, "I'm sure the doctor told you to get off your feet."

While chewing her food Wanda nodded and said, "Yes, she did."

Struggling Ben tried to slide over in the bed.

Pointing at the bed with his left hand he said, "You think you and the baby can fit right here!"

Smiling Wanda said, "I think we can fit!"

Even though Wanda was five feet six inches tall, it was hard for her to climb on the tall hospital bed. Her belly kept getting in the way, but she was determined.

Shaking his head, Ben smiled and said, "Sweetheart, I can't help you!"

Smiling Wanda said, "I can do it!"

When she finally got in the bed, she kissed her husband. She turned her back to him and snuggled as close as she could. Due to exhaustion she quickly fell asleep. Shortly after, the nurse came in to check on Ben. She found Ben and Wanda sleeping next to each other in the bed with his left arm lying on Wanda's belly. The nurse covered them up with a blanket and let them sleep.

6

THE COMMUNITY COMES TOGETHER

The TV news and newspaper reported 'local business man sacrifices his life to protect wife and unborn child during robbery' on every channel. The gunman was wanted for other robberies in the surrounding areas. Cason's Sporting Goods store was the only store with a video camera. However, once captured, he was identified by other victims. He was going to jail for a very long time. Mr. Jennings and Timothy Stevens visited Ben early the next morning.

As they walked into the room, Ben smiled and said, "Good morning!"

Mr. Jennings said, "Ben, you gave us quite a scare."

Smiling Ben said, "God continues to bless."

Timothy Stevens asked, "How is Wanda?"

Ben said, "She's great. She just went to the cafeteria to get something to eat."

Mr. Jennings said, "The video footage from the store captured everything. It's been running on all of the news channels."

Timothy said, "Man, to see you fly through the air and take that bullet was very emotional."

Ben said, "It was pure reflex. I could not let him shoot Wanda."

Mr. Jennings said, "I'm very proud of you. I have already contacted the police department and the court system. If they need anything, they will contact me first. I need to get depositions from both of you concerning what happened."

Ben said, "No problem, hopefully we can come by on Friday. Thanks for coming by to see me. I hope to get out of here tomorrow."

Timothy asked, "How does the shoulder feel?"

Touching his left shoulder with his right-hand Ben said, "It hurts! I'm trying not to use the morphine that much. The doctor said with physical therapy, I should be able to regain full function."

Mr. Jennings laughed and said, "I believe in pain medicine. If you need it, use it! We won't keep you. We just wanted to check on you. Do you need anything?"

Ben said, "The store in Macon is doing well. I do need someone to check on them for me."

Timothy said, "No problem. I will drive up there today. I have a client in Macon that I meet with every Friday. I can stop by the store and check out their processes then for you until you're better."

Ben said, "That would be a great help. Wanda said that she could do it, but I don't want to put that on her. She has ten weeks left before delivery."

Mr. Jennings asked, "Is there anything else you need?"

Ben said, "No sir, I'm fine."

Mr. Jennings said, "Oh! The building to the left of the store is available for purchase!"

Leaning forward Ben exclaimed, "I want it! I would love to build me and Wanda offices and possibly a daycare area for employees that need child care."

Timothy said, "That's a great idea. I will put in an offer for the building."

Ben said, "Thanks!"

Wanda walked into the room. Mr. Jennings and Timothy gave her a hug.

Wanda said, "I'm glad you were able to stop by."

Timothy said, "You know we had to check on our favorite couple."

Smiling Wanda said, "He's doing so much better today. I am grateful."

Mr. Jennings said, "I understand that you have ten weeks left."

Wanda smiled and said, "Yes, we're very excited."

Mr. Jennings said, "My wife wants to have you all over for dinner again next week."

Ben said, "That sounds great!"

Wanda said, "I would like that!"

Mr. Jennings said, "We will finalize a date this weekend!"

Ben said, "Sounds good!"

Timothy said, "I'll be in touch. Wanda, take care of him!"

Smiling Wanda said, "You know I will."

Mr. Jennings and Timothy Stevens left the room.

Ben asked, "Did you find anything you wanted to eat?"

Wanda said, "Yes, I bought a yogurt!"

Ben smiled. Just as Wanda was sitting down to eat her yogurt, her parents walked in.

Momma asked, "Ben, Wanda, how are you two?"

After hugging her mother, Wanda said, "Momma, we're fine today!"

Dad said, "Ben, you scared us to death."

Smiling Ben said, "I'm so sorry to worry you."

Momma said, "The video is all over the news. Every channel you turn to, you see the video of Ben flying through the air taking the bullet with you crouched down behind the register."

Wanda said, "We haven't seen it."

Dad said, "The reporter said that the gunman robbed other stores in the surrounding area, but your store was the only one that had video. This guy will be going to jail for a long time."

Ben said, "I'm glad. When the silent alarm went off, my first thought was that it was pressed by mistake. When I walked into the shopping area, I immediately saw Wanda, then I saw the gunman."

Wanda said, "When the man told me to put the money in a bag, I was able to press the alarm. I tried to remain calm, but it was not easy. I was surprisingly calm, but I was also afraid."

Ben said, "I was walking as fast as I could to get to the front of the store. By the time I got there, he was already unraveling."

Wanda said, "Ben was very calm, he tried to talk to the man. The man was so angry. I had not done anything to cause him to want to shoot me, but he was determined to pull that trigger."

Momma said, "I get nervous every time I think about what could have happened."

Looking at his wife, Dad said, "But it didn't! Thank you, Ben, for protecting our daughter."

Ben said, "I can't lose her! She means the world to me!"

Wanda leaned over to kiss him.

Momma asked, "Do you need anything?"

Wanda said, "No, not really. I slept good last night. The baby and I are fine."

Dad said, "Good, we will be here for two nights, unless you need us longer."

Wanda said, "That's great! We're hoping Ben will be released tomorrow."

Ben said, "Wanda has been in this hospital with me since yesterday. If you could get her to go home and take a break, that would be great."

Wanda said, "Good try! I'm not leaving you!"

Dad said, "Man, that was a good try. I know my daughter, she's not leaving this hospital until you leave!"

Ben laughed!

The day went by fast. Ben and Wanda talked and laughed all day. Wanda learned how to dress his wound and change the bandages. Dr. Holmes stopped by to see how Wanda and the baby were doing.

Dr. Holmes exclaimed, "Wanda, you look great today!"

Wanda said, "I feel great!"

Dr. Holmes asked, "Are you having any more cramps?"

Concerned Ben interjected, "Wanda, you didn't tell me, you were having cramps!"

Wanda said, "Truthfully, I forgot about them."

Dr. Holmes said, "It was probably from all of the excitement yesterday. When she settled down, the baby settled down."

Leaning forward Ben asked, "Doctor, are you sure?"

Dr. Holmes said, "Yes! I would be concerned if she was not doing so well today."

Looking at Ben Wanda said, "I am fine."

Dr. Holmes said, "I know you have been running, but for these last ten weeks, I don't want you to do more than walk."

Wanda said, "No problem. Can I walk five miles?"

Dr. Holmes said, "Slowly, a stroll, not a fast walk!"

Ben said, "I will walk with her to slow her down."

Dr. Holmes laughed.

Wanda said, "I feel good, the baby is very active. It has been kicking all morning."

Dr. Holmes said, "That's just an indication that it is growing. It's trying to find space to stretch out."

Ben said, "Dr. Holmes, we know that you know the sex of the baby. We appreciate you not telling us."

Wanda said, "Well, the way this baby is kicking, I think it's a boy!"

Ben said, "It could be a girl soccer player!"

Dr. Holmes laughed!

Wanda said, "I will see you for our regular appointment in two weeks!"

Dr. Holmes said, "That would be great. Ben, how is the shoulder?"

Ben said, "It hurts! Overall, I am fine."

Dr. Holmes said, "The video is all over the news!"

Wanda said, "We heard. We haven't seen it yet."

Dr. Holmes said, "Ben, it is a beautiful display of love. I am glad that I know you both!"

Wanda hugged her and said, "God has blessed me!"

Dr. Holmes said, "Yes, he has!"

Finally, on the next day Ben was released from the hospital. Wanda took him straight home. Ben was happy to be home. He walked around the house like he had been gone for weeks.

Ben exclaimed, "I'm so glad to be home!"

Wanda said, "Me too! It seems like we've been gone for a really long time."

Ben hugged his wife and said, "You know that I worry about you."

Wanda said, "I worry about you too!"

Ben said, "I know that our second anniversary is coming up soon. Do you want to go to the condo?"

Wanda said, "No, I think we should stay local until the baby is born."

Ben said, "Great idea. David said that he would cook us a romantic dinner if we want."

Wanda said, "No, I just want to spend the whole day with you by ourselves."

Smiling Ben said, "That sounds like a wonderful idea."

The doorbell rang. Wanda rushed to the door. Ben went into the kitchen to get some water to drink. Wanda opened the door. Standing at the door was Mrs. Agnes Boatwright.

Wanda said, "Mrs. Boatwright! How are you? Please come in!"

Stepping inside Mrs. Boatwright said, "I saw your car when you pulled up. I just wanted to stop by and make sure you both were OK."

Ben walked into the room and said, "Hello Mrs. Boatwright!"

Mrs. Boatwright asked, "Ben, how is your shoulder?"

Ben said, "It is getting better. Wanda takes great care of me."

Mrs. Boatwright said, "That's because you take great care of her. I made you some blackberry jam. I have won blue ribbons for this jam; I hope you like it."

Wanda took the basket of jam and said, "Thank you so much. We love blackberry jam."

Ben said, "Thank you. How is your dog, Buttons, doing?"

Mrs. Boatwright said, "He is doing much better, I can't let him out as much as I want to. He keeps coming over here."

Wanda said, "That's not a problem, we don't mind."

Mrs. Boatwright said, "Thank you for saying that. I finally figured out that there's a stray cat loose in the neighborhood.

That cat likes to lay in your driveway. That's why my dog keeps coming over here."

Ben laughed and asked, "Mrs. Boatwright, would you like to have a seat? We are just getting home."

Mrs. Boatwright said, "Thank you, but not this time. I have been waiting for you to come home. I wanted to apologize for the mean things I said to you and about you. I did not mean them when I said them. I was just being stubborn. I can see why Mr. Cason loved you Ben; you're a wonderful, young man."

In shock Ben said, "Thank you ma'am."

Wanda said, "Mrs. Boatwright, we would love it if you would come to dinner on Friday night. That will give Ben a chance to rest."

Mrs. Boatwright said, "I would be honored."

Ben said, "Great, please bring Buttons with you!"

Wanda asked, "Would six o'clock be OK?"

Mrs. Boatwright said, "I will see you at six o'clock. I will go now."

Wanda opened the door and walked Mrs. Boatwright to the driveway.

Mrs. Boatwright said, "The two of you make a beautiful couple."

Wanda said, "Thank you, we love each other very much!"

Mrs. Boatwright asked, "It is obvious. When are you due?"

Wanda said, "Less than ten more weeks!"

Mrs. Boatwright said, "I will see you on Friday."

Wanda waved and walked back into the house.

Ben asked, "What was that?"

Wanda said, "I don't know. She was very nice. When we were in the driveway, she was even nicer."

Ben said, "God answers prayer!"

Wanda hugged Ben and said, "Yes, he does!"

Ben and Wanda had dinner and went for a walk. All of the neighbors were outside asking how they were doing. Most of the neighbors had always been nice, but this was over the top. After the walk, Ben and Wanda sat on the porch thanking God for changing the hearts of their neighbors.

On Friday, Ben and Wanda stopped by Mr. Jennings' office to give their deposition. Mr. Jennings finalized dinner plans for Tuesday night. They stopped by the store. Everyone was so glad to see Ben and Wanda when they walked in. They were very happy to see all of their team members. The wall still needed to be repaired, where the gunman shot and missed Wanda.

Ben said, "We need to repair that wall."

Wanda said, "Let's leave it there for a little while."

Ben asked, "It doesn't bother you? I don't want you to feel uncomfortable in the store."

Wanda said, "No, it's a constant reminder that God allowed the gunman to miss the first time. When you couldn't be there, God was!"

Ben leaned over and kissed his wife. Uncle Robert debriefed them on what was going on in the store.

Uncle Robert said, "The store has become a tourist attraction. People from all over want to see. While they are here, they buy things. We have sold more in the last two days, than we did all last week."

Ben said, "What Satan meant for harm, God has worked it out for our good!"

Uncle Robert said, "Everything else is going smoothly. I may need to hire two more people."

Wanda said, "When we walked in, you were smiling. What's going on?"

Uncle Robert asked, "Have you talked to Dee?"

Wanda said, "No! Is everything OK?"

Uncle Robert said, "David asked her to be his girlfriend!"

Ben exclaimed, "It's about time!"

Wanda said, "I know that she's elated."

Uncle Robert said, "I am too! It's obvious that he cares about her. I know he was concerned about her going off to college this fall."

Wanda said, "I know. I'm glad they are finally a couple."

Ben said, "Fourth of July is coming up, this year it's on a Saturday. Let's do a big celebration for the employees and family."

Wanda said, "That's a great idea. We can have it behind the celebration center."

Uncle Robert said, "I know a guy that can cater barbeque for us."

Ben said, "I know, it's only three weeks away. You think, we can pull it off."

Wanda said, "I think so! I will start making a list!"

Uncle Robert said, "We can close the store at one o'clock, so everyone can attend."

Ben said, "That would be great."

That evening, Mrs. Boatwright and Buttons came to dinner. Wanda prepared a delicious meal. She cooked baked chicken, vegetable rice pilaf, and English peas.

Mrs. Boatwright said, "This was a delicious dinner."

Wanda said, "Thank you. My cooking is getting better."

Ben said, "Don't listen to her, she's a great cook."

Mrs. Boatwright said, "My husband cooked a lot before he died. I miss him."

Ben asked, "How did he die?"

Mrs. Boatwright said, "He was in a car accident. He was hit by a drunk driver. That driver was a black man."

Wanda said, "I am so sorry to hear that."

Ben asked, "Is that why you were so mean to me?"

Mrs. Boatwright said, "Yes. I have never interacted with many people of different races. Truthfully, I realized the other day that I had been stereotyping. Every bad thing that I heard about a black person, I believed it. When my husband was killed, I was very angry. I took that anger out on every black person I met. For that I am sorry."

Ben said, "I'm glad that you realized that we're all the same."

Mrs. Boatwright said, "I am too. When I accused you of trying to steal my dog, deep down I knew that you were not trying to steal Buttons. It was easier for me to accept that you intended harm to me instead of believing that my dog was chasing after a cat."

Everyone laughed.

Wanda said, "Mrs. Boatwright, what changed your mind?"

Mrs. Boatwright said, "I told you the other day that I saw the stray cat in the yard. Even after I saw the stray cat, I still wanted to be angry."

Ben and Wanda gave Mrs. Boatwright their full attention.

Mrs. Boatwright said, "After I saw the video of Ben risking his life for you, I realized that for him to do that, he must not have any malice in his heart. My husband would have risked his life for me. I also realized that my husband would be very ashamed of the way I have been living. I have been very sanctimonious."

Ben and Wanda smiled.

Mrs. Boatwright said, "So again, I am sorry for my behavior. I have also called all of our neighbors and apologized. I was wrong to vilify you."

Ben said, "We appreciate that!"

Wanda said, "I made some dessert. I used some of your blackberry jam to make thumbprint cookies."

Mrs. Boatwright said, "You know, I never thought of that!"

Ben said, "They are delicious! I had some earlier."

Looking down at her dog, Mrs. Boatwright said, "I can see that Buttons, enjoyed his dinner too. You're going to spoil him."

Wanda said, "We spoil people that we love."

Mrs. Boatwright smiled and said, "I do too!"

Everyone laughed.

Mrs. Boatwright asked, "May I take some of these cookies with me?"

Getting up from the table Wanda said, "Of course, I will pack some for you."

Mrs. Boatwright said, "OK! Next week, you are invited to my house for dinner."

Ben said, "You don't have to do that!"

Mrs. Boatwright said, "I want too. I'm not as good a cook as Wanda, but I can cook a few things."

Wanda said, "We look forward to it."

Ben said, "Wanda likes to walk in the evening. If you like, we can take Buttons with us, so he can get some exercise."

Mrs. Boatwright said, "I would really appreciate that."

Ben and Wanda walked Mrs. Boatwright and Buttons home. Everyone had a great time.

The next week was filled with dinner invitations. Dinner at the Jennings was very nice. Wanda and Ben enjoyed spending time with them. Judge Jennings was always the center of attention. He had stories that made you laugh and cry.

Dinner at Mrs. Boatwright was just as nice. Her house was filled with southern trinkets. She prepared breakfast for dinner. She served grits, eggs, bacon, sausage, and biscuits with blackberry jam.

Wanda said, "I never thought of having breakfast for dinner."

Mrs. Boatwright laughed and said, "My husband worked during the night. When he came home, he went straight to bed. So, we did not have breakfast during the morning hours."

Ben said, "This is delicious."

Wanda asked, "Is that a picture of your husband?"

Mrs. Boatwright got up from the table to retrieve the framed photo.

Wanda said, "That's a great picture."

Mrs. Boatwright said, "Yes, we got married when I was eighteen years old. He was twenty-five. We were only married twenty years, when he died."

Ben said, "I'm sure you have some great memories."

Mrs. Boatwright said, "I do. However, being a young, angry widow is not easy."

Wanda asked, "Did you have any children?"

Mrs. Boatwright said, "Yes, we had a son. Unfortunately, he died while on active duty in the army."

Ben said, "I'm sorry to hear that!"

Wanda asked, "Did he have any children?"

Mrs. Boatwright said, "No, he didn't. He and his girlfriend had planned to get married."

Wanda said, "Well, Mrs. Boatwright, your lonely days are over. Ben and I officially adopt you into our family."

Ben smiled and said, "We would love for you to meet the rest of our family."

Surprised Mrs. Boatwright said, "Wow! You two are so loving. I would love to meet the rest of your family."

7

TIME TO CELEBRATE

The Fourth of July celebration was awesome. The food was delicious, the temperature was eighty-eight degrees, and everyone had a great time. The city of Fairville had a firework display scheduled for nine o'clock that night. The view from the celebration center was fantastic. People finally left around ten o'clock. Everyone helped clean up before they left. It was a great celebration.

Mrs. Boatwright attended the barbeque and had a wonderful time. She could not remember the last time, she attended a barbeque. She and Mom got along so well. They made plans to go to Bingo on Thursday nights. Dee and David were inseparable. Whenever, David catered an event, Dee was there. David made sure she was involved in every aspect of the café and his spaghetti sauce.

Dee received a scholarship to cover her tuition. Uncle Robert was happy, that lessened his out of pocket expenses. Mary was excited about going back to the University of Georgia for her second year. Wow, how time flies. Her university was sponsoring an international trip to Spain for three weeks in

October. Students, that participated, would receive credit toward their current classes. Mary was excited. Her first international trip. She applied for her passport and expected it to arrive before she left for college in August.

She planned to share a room again with Eva. They had become great friends. Becky was attending Middle Georgia State University. She and Mary were still close friends. The baby was due the second week of August. Deep down Wanda knew that it would be early, but she did not want to alarm Ben. Ben was going to physical therapy three times a week. Even though he hated it, he was determined to get his full range of motion and function again.

The women at the church gave Wanda a baby shower, she was overwhelmed. The baby's room was finally ready. Wanda and Ben agreed to give birth naturally. They attended classes. They felt ready. Instead of gaining weight, Wanda was losing weight. Dr. Holmes wanted her to intake more calories. Wanda felt that she could not eat any more.

Early one morning Ben asked, "What would you like for breakfast?"

Wanda said, "I know I need to eat, but it's hard. I just don't have an appetite."

Ben said, "The baby does!"

Wanda said, "I know. How about French toast with sausage?"

Ben smiled and said, "That sounds delicious. If you promise to eat more than a mote, I will go start breakfast."

Wanda laughed and said, "I promise. You're doing good with just one arm!"

Smiling Ben said, "As long as I have one to hold you, I'm fine!"

Wanda smiled and said, "Ben, I know you said, it doesn't matter to you if the baby is a boy or a girl."

Ben said, "It doesn't!"

Wanda said, "Deep down, I want a boy! I want to name him Benjamin James Davis, Jr. I want him to grow up and be just like his father."

Ben smiled and said, "I was thinking we could have a beautiful, little girl that will grow up to be just like her mother!"

Wanda smiled, "Too bad we aren't having twins!"

Ben laughed and said, "Now, that would be a little much for me. I'm ready for one at a time!"

Wanda laughed. Then she felt a deep pain in her back.

Ben saw the expression on her face and asked, "Wanda, what's wrong?"

Wanda asked, "Ben, what is today's date?"

Ben laughed and said proudly, "It's July 29, 1981. Why?"

Wanda said, "I think it is the birth date of our baby."

Stepping closer Ben asked, "Are you sure?"

Wanda said, "I think so. I had some contractions last night. Just then, I had a major one."

Ben grabbed his stop watch and said, "Let's see how far apart the contractions are."

Wanda said, "OK, please go ahead and put my suit case in the car, just in case."

Ben ran to put the suitcase in the car. Wanda figured she better go ahead and get dressed. When Ben came back, Wanda was leaning over the bed.

Ben asked, "Another contraction?"

Wanda said, "Yes!"

Ben said, "That was not even three minutes. I guess you're right, it's time to go to the hospital. I'll call Dr. Holmes first."

Ben made the necessary calls. Wanda got dressed and was

trying to put on her sneakers. Ben grabbed some slip-on sandals and gave them to her. Before they could make it to the car, Wanda had another contraction.

Ben said, "Wanda, I can't pick you up yet. You have to make it to the car."

Determined Wanda said, "I know. I can make it."

It took all that she had, but she made it to the car. Ben drove very carefully to the hospital. When they arrived, Dr. Holmes was waiting with a nurse at the entrance. He drove up and they got Wanda out of the car.

Dr. Holmes commanded, "Ben, park the car! We will start prepping her."

Ben parked the car. Before he got out of the car, he took time to pray.

He said, "God, I thank you for all that you have done for me. I thank you for my wife and child. Lord, I ask that you allow this child to be healthy and allow Wanda to deliver without any complications. In Jesus name I pray. Amen!"

When Ben entered the hospital, he was escorted to the fourth floor. They prepped him for the delivery room. Ben realized that he was not nervous, he was ready. He was ready to meet his baby. He was ready for them to be a family.

A medical assistant escorted Ben to the delivery room. Wanda was already there. He sat down in the chair provided and kissed his wife as lovingly as he could.

Wanda said, "Ben, I love you!"

Ben said, "I love you more. Today is the day!"

Wanda said, "I know! Are you nervous?"

Ben said, "No, not at all. I'm ready."

Wanda said, "I am too! I may have to accept some drugs. These pains are horrible."

Dr. Holmes said, "Wanda, unfortunately it's too late for drugs. We have to do this naturally."

Wanda laughed.

Ben said, "I'm right here with you. We can do this!"

Wanda smiled and said, "Yes, we can!"

Dr. Holmes exclaimed, "Wanda, you have already dilated seven centimeters. This is going to be quick."

Wanda asked, "Will there be a problem since this is three weeks early?"

Dr. Holmes said, "It should not be. Depending on the weight, the baby may have to stay in the hospital a few days."

Ben said, "Everything is going to be fine. God has brought us to this point. He will take us through it."

Wanda tried to smile. She was sweating. Ben wiped her forehead. Next thing you knew it was time.

Dr. Holmes said, "Wanda, I need you to give me three good pushes. Ready for the first!"

Wanda tried to breathe, the pain was intense.

Dr. Holmes said, "OK, push now!"

Wanda did.

Dr. Holmes said, "Relax. Get ready for the next one. According to my monitor, you have about thirty seconds to rest."

Ben prayed. He wiped Wanda's forehead again.

Dr. Holmes said, "Get ready for the next one. Push!"

Straining, Wanda did.

Dr. Holmes exclaimed, "I can see the head. We are almost there."

Ben said, "Wanda, I love you very much!"

Wanda smiled. Ben had never seen such big droplets of sweat, he wiped her forehead again.

Dr. Holmes said, "OK, Wanda, I think this will be the last one. Get ready."

Ben held Wanda's hand. Wanda was ready.

Dr. Holmes said, "Ready, push!"

Wanda pushed as hard as she could. Next thing she heard was the baby crying.

Dr. Holmes said, "You did it. Congratulations, you have a baby boy!"

Wanda cried. Ben cried. The baby was crying. Dr. Holmes laid the baby on Wanda's chest.

Ben said, "We have a son!"

Wanda said, "And his name is Ben!"

Ben cut the umbilical cord and the nurse took the baby to clean him up. Tears could not stop flowing down the cheeks of both Wanda and Ben. They were so happy that their son was finally here, healthy and whole. His lungs were strong, he had a head full of curly hair. He was twenty-one inches long and weighed six pounds and nine ounces. As soon as little Ben was cleaned up, the nurse laid him on Wanda's chest.

Wanda said, "I feel like my heart is about to burst. I have so much love in it."

Ben said, "I feel the same way. I can't stop crying."

Wanda said, "Ben, he looks a little like you."

Ben smiled and said, "I see you in him!"

They laughed.

Ben said, "I guess I need to go call everyone. Are you OK?"

Wanda said, "I'm fine. They will be moving us to a room soon."

Ben kissed his wife and then kissed his son on his head. When he entered the hallway, he saw a pay phone on the wall. He called his mom, Wanda's parents, and Uncle Robert to spread the news. He then called Mr. Jennings, Mrs. Boatwright,

Caleb, Paul, and Tammy's parents. Everyone was so happy that little Ben was healthy and finally here. When Ben arrived in the hospital room, he saw Wanda breast feeding little Ben. He placed Wanda's suitcase on the chair.

Wanda said, "He's hungry."

Ben asked, "How do you feel?"

Wanda said, "Right now, I'm numb."

Ben said, "I bought you a coke!"

Wanda said, "Thank you so much! You're always thinking of me."

Ben said, "I always will."

Wanda asked, "Are you OK?"

Ben said, "I'm fine. I'm so thankful that God saved you for me. My cup runneth over!"

Wanda said, "You know I feel the same way. Sometimes, I don't think I'm doing enough to show you how much you mean to me."

Ben said, "It's obvious in everything you say and do. I know."

Wanda said, "Good!"

Ben laughed.

Wanda said, "I hope they release us both on tomorrow, maybe Wednesday. Dr. Holmes said that the baby was fine. She was shocked how much he weighed, all of his reflexes are fine."

Ben said, "I'm glad. I called everyone. Everyone is elated that you and Ben are doing well. They are spreading the word."

Wanda said, "When you go home tonight…"

Ben interrupted, "I'm not going anywhere. I'll be right here with you."

Wanda said, "I did not pack anything for you."

Ben said, "I packed a suitcase for me. It's been in the car for months."

Wanda laughed and reached for him.

Wanda asked, "Are you ready to hold your son?"

Reluctantly Ben said, "I don't think so. My left arm is not strong enough yet to lift him up from you. I can wait. Maybe later when you're up, I can sit in the chair and you can place him in my arm."

Getting out of bed Wanda said, "I am ready to do that now. Have a seat!"

Ben smiled and sat down.

Wanda placed the baby in Ben's right arm. Tears rolled down his cheeks.

Wanda asked, "How does that feel?"

Ben smiled and said, "Indescribable."

Wanda said, "I need to take a picture. Let me get my camera."

Wanda retrieved her camera and took a picture of her wonderful husband holding their beautiful child.

Dr. Holmes walked in and said, "That's a nice picture. Let me take one of all three of you."

Wanda passed the camera to Dr. Holmes and said, "I'm sure I look a mess, but I don't care!"

Ben said, "You're as beautiful as always!"

Dr. Holmes took the picture and passed the camera back to Wanda.

Dr. Holmes said, "OK, Wanda back in bed. I need you to take it easy for a little while. You can get up when you need to, but try to stay in bed as much as possible."

Wanda said, "I feel fine."

Dr. Holmes said, "That's great. I want you and the baby to stay in the hospital for two nights. I just want to monitor you both. Today is Monday, so hopefully you can be released on Wednesday."

Wanda said, "I expected that! Ben will be spending the night with us."

Dr. Holmes said, "Great, I will have a cot wheeled in here for you."

Wanda said, "That's not necessary. We're good at sharing a hospital bed."

Everyone laughed.

Dr. Holmes said, "I will check on you tomorrow. Little Ben looks very content."

Ben said, "Well, we know that his lungs work when he's not content!"

Everyone laughed.

As Dr. Holmes was walking out of the door, Mom, Mary, David, and Dee were walking in.

Mom said, "Oh my goodness. He is beautiful!"

Mary said, "I'm an aunt. I think I want him to call me Auntie Mary. I like that better than Aunt Mary!"

Everyone laughed.

David asked, "Did everything go OK during the delivery?"

Wanda said, "It was very quick. From the time we left home until the time he was born was about two hours."

Mom said, "That was quick."

Dee asked, "Was it painful?"

Wanda said, "Extremely! However, it was worth it!"

Mary said, "Ben, you're holding him very good with one arm!"

Ben said, "I'm very nervous. This is just another reason why I have to get my arm back to full operation."

Mom said, "It takes time. It has only been six weeks since you had surgery. Don't rush the healing process."

Dee said, "He's a beautiful baby. He looks like Wanda and Ben mixed together!"

Everyone laughed.

Mary said, "He does have Ben's nose, but he has Wanda's lips!"

Everyone laughed.

Mom said, "He's beautiful. I'm a grandmother!"

Dee asked, "What do you want little Ben to call you?"

Mom said, "I don't know. I like grandma, but since he has another grandmother too. I don't want to be selfish."

Ben said, "Well, when he starts to talk, we can figure it out then."

Mary said, "Hopefully, he will talk early like I did!"

Everyone laughed.

David said, "Well, right now. I'm his only uncle. I feel special!"

Mary said, "I'm so glad he was born before I left to go back to school. I did not want to miss this."

Wanda said, "I was praying that he would arrive while you and Dee were here."

Dee said, "David is taking me to tour Middle Georgia State University campus tomorrow."

Ben said, "That's great. It seems like a long time ago when we went to visit in 1975 with Grandpa. So much has happened since then. It has only been six years, but I have graduated, gotten my masters, gotten married, and now have a son. Wow!"

Mom said, "That's life. It stands still for no one. I now have two sons that have graduated from college, a daughter in her second year, retired from one job and totally enjoying another. I have a daughter in law and a grandson. God has blessed."

Wanda said, "Yes, he has!"

Dee said, "Well, I now have a boyfriend, whom I adore."

Mary said, "You're right, it took three years for him to figure it out!"

Everyone laughed.

Pulling Dee close to him, David said, "Yes, I'm a little slow, but I figured it out! I'm glad that I did!"

Ben asked, "How is construction going?"

David said, "It's going well. We have picked out all of the colors, furniture, displays, appliances and everything else. Frank McCants is doing a great job. I'm glad I was able to buy the building next door. Now, we can have a larger kitchen and storage area."

Wanda said, "That was a great idea. When do you expect to open?"

David said, "Dee thinks we should open the Saturday of Labor Day weekend."

Dee said, "Then I can be home for the long weekend."

Mom said, "That's a great idea."

Mary said, "I'm so sad that I will miss it."

Wanda said, "I will send you pictures. Oh! Dee, please look in the hallway to see if you see anyone that can take a picture of all of us."

Dee stepped in the hallway and returned with a nurse. The nurse took a picture of the entire family. Wanda sat on Ben's knee, holding baby Ben. Everyone stood behind. It was a beautiful picture."

Mom said, "Wanda, I want a copy of that one!"

Wanda laughed!

Mom said, "Well, we're not going to stay long. We will check on you later today. Wanda, please try to take a nap. I know you feel good, but your body has gone through a lot delivering this bundle of joy."

Wanda said, "I will try!"

Mom said, "Because when you get home, it is going to be non-stop!"

Ben said confidently, "Well, I figured between the two of us, we can handle a baby!"

Mom laughed and said, "Don't be so sure!"

Everyone laughed.

8

GRAND OPENING OF THE CAFÉ

The next two days flew by. There were constant visitors to see baby Ben. Wanda took pictures of everyone oohing and awing over the baby. She knew that when she got home, she could not come out until the baby was six weeks old.

Mom said, "I know you think it's an overkill. Your body needs to heal and the baby needs to build up an immunity before you bring him back out into the world. So, in six weeks after you take him to his first doctor's appointment, then you can start taking him places."

Wanda said, "My mom told me the same thing. I don't mind. I'd rather be safe than sorry."

Ben asked, "Does that mean we can't take him out for a walk?"

Mom said, "Yes, that baby does not need to come back outside for six weeks?"

Wanda laughed and said, "Now, that's going to be hard!"

Ben and Wanda took their bundle of joy home. Wanda sat in the backseat with the baby strapped in the car seat. Ben tried to drive slowly, Wanda's body was sore. When they arrived home, Buttons was in the driveway. Ben got out of the car and moved Buttons to the porch. He then parked the car.

Mrs. Boatwright walked over to retrieve Buttons and said, "I don't know what we are going to do about Buttons in your driveway."

Ben laughed.

Ben opened the passenger door for Wanda to get out. Wanda unstrapped Ben from the car seat and stood by the car.

Mrs. Boatwright oohed and said, "Oh, he is adorable."

Smiling Wanda said, "He is!"

Mrs. Boatwright said, "When I had my son, they wouldn't let me come out of the house for six weeks and not many people could hold the baby."

Ben laughed and said, "Our mothers have demanded the same thing."

Mrs. Boatwright said, "Well, please obey. It's for the baby's protection. Wanda, do you need anything?"

Wanda said, "No ma'am. We're fine and very excited."

Mrs. Boatwright said, "You both are glowing with happiness. I will stop by to check on you tomorrow. I'll also let the neighborhood know the good news and let them know you're keeping the baby isolated for six weeks before everyone can see."

Ben said, "Mrs. Boatwright, you've established a neighborhood network! Thanks!"

Mrs. Boatwright grabbed Buttons, laughed and said, "I'm not being imperious. I'm using my powers for good now!"

Ben and Wanda laughed and went into the house.

Wanda said, "We are home! This is where you'll be raised and loved."

Ben asked, "Are you nervous?"

Wanda said, "No, I feel confident."

Ben said, "I do too. If we raise him with our morals and values, teaching him how to love and serve God and others, he'll be fine."

Wanda said, "I know he will!"

The first few nights went by fast, all baby Ben did was sleep. Wanda put the baby on a schedule and it seemed to work. Baby Ben was hungry every two hours. It seemed like Wanda never slept. Ben made sure he got up whenever Wanda was up.

Wanda said, "Ben, you can go back to bed!"

Wiping his eyes Ben said, "No, I want to experience everything. I don't have to go to work, so we can sleep when Ben sleeps!"

Wanda laughed!

Ben asked, "How do you feel?"

Wanda said, "My body is not as sore as it was. So that's good. My stomach is going down, I'm thankful for that. I hope that I can return to my pre-baby weight."

Ben smiled and said, "I need to return to my pre-baby weight too!"

Wanda laughed and said, "You look stronger!"

Ben said, "When I'm at rehab, I have been working out my right side too with heavier weights."

Wanda laughed!

Ben asked, "Why do you think Ben keeps waking up?"

Wanda said, "He's hungry! I don't think I'm producing enough milk for him?"

Walking closer to her Ben asked, "What can we do?"

Wanda said, "I don't know yet. I plan to ask our mothers later today!"

Ben said, "Good! Well, looks like he has fallen asleep again."

Wanda said, "Good, maybe we can sleep for two hours."

Wanda laid the baby in the bassinet and got back in bed. She snuggled up to her husband and they both quickly fell asleep.

Both mothers advised Wanda to keep up the schedule of feeding the baby every two hours. Her body would adapt and start to produce more milk. Then she would be able to extend the feedings to three hours, then hopefully four.

The next few weeks flew by. Ben continued physical therapy. He initiated plans to start the renovation of the building next to the store. Uncle Robert continued to do a great job at the store. He also volunteered to check on the store in Macon once a week. He and Charlene were very happy. They were ecstatic that Dee was living on campus.

Mom and Mrs. Boatwright had become very good friends. When Mom needed help at the event center, Mrs. Boatwright and Miss Bessie were there to help. All three of them were very close and enjoyed Bingo every Thursday night and walked in the park on Saturday mornings.

David still lived at home, but he was seldom there. He was busy catering, renovating the café, and making trips to Atlanta concerning his spaghetti sauce. His spaghetti sauce was now available all over the United States. For the first year, it was only available in the southeast region. However, it did so well, it was now being distributed to every major grocery store. David was well on his way to becoming a millionaire.

The time had come for the grand opening of his café. It had also been six weeks since little Ben was born. Wanda was so thankful that she and the baby could leave the house.

David's café was called David's Soups, Sandwiches, and Desserts. Everyone was very proud of him. David hired three servers and one cook to help in the kitchen. The café would only be open on Tuesday through Saturday from nine in the morning to five in the afternoon. However, for the grand opening, it would be open that Saturday, Sunday, and Monday of Labor Day weekend.

Mom was very proud. Both of her sons were doing well. Her daughter was taking the University of Georgia by storm. She was excelling in all of her classes and had petitioned for an additional international trip to France in the spring.

During the grand opening of the café, David gave away free cupcakes, sandwiches, and cups of soup. He had a table for people to sign up for his mailing list to receive future coupons. He had a different table for people who wanted to place future orders for cakes or other desserts. David and Dee took a beautiful picture standing in front of the café.

Baby Ben was adored by all. Wanda had dropped most of her baby weight. Ben and Wanda pushed baby Ben around town in the stroller. It was a beautiful day. As they walked through town, they discussed other things they could do for the town of Fairville.

Wanda said, "I'm glad the sports complex is finally finished. It took longer to build than I expected."

Ben said, "You're right. I didn't expect it to take two years, but it's finished. Now, the youth will have intramural sport teams that they can get involved in all year long. What do you think we should do next?"

Wanda said, "Well, we're working on the office building. We'll have offices for us and some to lease out in there."

Ben said, "We will also have a daycare area for employees of the store."

Wanda said, "Maybe depending on enrollment, we can open it up to other parents."

Ben said, "That's a great idea. That building will also have a kitchen, so food can be prepared on site."

Wanda said, "We have entertainment for the city taken care

of. We have built the sports complex for exercise. Something intellectual would be great."

Ben asked, "What about an auditorium, where plays and concerts can be performed."

Wanda said, "That's thinking big. Are you talking about an auditorium that will hold maybe 500 people or a stadium that holds thousands?"

Ben laughed and said, "I was thinking an auditorium that would hold 500 to 1,000 people. Neighboring cities could also use it. The school can hold graduations there."

Wanda said, "That's a good idea!"

Ben said, "I've been thinking about other sporting goods stores. Mr. Jennings told me that we could sell franchises. We would not have to do the work, but people who wanted to piggy back off of our success would have the opportunity."

Wanda said, "I don't know much about franchises. Let me do some research."

Ben said, "OK! Let's keep thinking, we don't have to decide today."

Wanda said, "I was thinking about going back on birth control."

Ben asked, "For how long?"

Wanda said, "I was thinking just until Ben is about eighteen months."

Kissing his wife, Ben said, "OK. I do want more children!"

Wanda smiled and said, "I do too!"

When they returned to the café, the line was still long. There had been a line of people all day. As soon as some were served, more people got in line. Dee started bringing samples to the crowd. Everyone was very happy with the food.

Ben said, "Looks like David and Dee have a successful café on their hands."

Wanda said, "I'm so happy for them. Look at them, they're glowing."

Uncle Robert and Auntie Charlene walked up to Ben and Wanda.

Uncle Robert said, "I never imagined Fairville having such a nice sandwich shop."

Auntie Charlene said, "Me neither. When I first arrived here, blacks were not allowed to go into the café. Now, the only café we have is owned by a black man."

Everyone laughed.

Ben said, "Grandpa told me several times that Fairville was changing for the better. He was right."

Leaning down to look at the baby Uncle Robert asked, "How is my great nephew doing?"

Wanda replied, "He's pure joy!"

Auntie Charlene said, "He's growing. You have him dressed so nicely."

Wanda said, "We received so many baby gifts and outfits. I have enough to dress him in something different every day. I'm just trying to put it on him before he out grows it."

Everyone laughed.

On Sunday, Ben, Wanda, and little Ben went to church. Everyone was so happy to see them and fussed over the baby. After the sermon, Reverend King called the family up and said a special prayer over them. He anointed the baby with oil and dedicated him to Christ.

Reverend King said, "I know this is not our traditional baby dedication service, but I feel the need to go ahead and dedicate this child. I know that normally we would have God parents. However, I know the love that all of us have for Ben and Wanda. Who with me would take the pledge to love, oversee, guide, and pray for baby Ben."

Every adult in the church stood up.

Reverend King said, "Ben, Wanda, our church is small, but we take a pledge to not only love, oversee, guide, and pray for your baby but to continue to keep you in our prayers. Anytime you need help, you have a church family you can come to. If we see that you need help, we promise not to bombard you, but to be there to assist you as you raise this child."

Tears were rolling down the cheeks of Ben and Wanda.

Ben said, "We can't thank you enough for your love and support."

Reverend King said, "Continue to let God lead you."

Ben and Wanda returned to their pew. After church, Ben and Wanda stayed longer to talk to everyone in the congregation. Little Ben slept through most of it. After church, they planned to go to the café for lunch. When they arrived, there was a line at least seventy-five people deep.

Wanda said, "Well, I guess we won't be having lunch at the café today!"

Ben said, "This is wonderful. I can't believe they still have a line."

Wanda said, "Let me take a picture of the people, then we can go through the back and just say hello."

Wanda took a picture then Ben drove to the back of the café. They entered the back door and found all of the staff scurrying to fill orders. David saw them and quickly gave them a hug.

Ben said, "Man, you got a winner going on here!"

David said, "I know. Dee and I have been here since six o'clock this morning. We prepped as much as we could. The staff came in at eight o'clock. We didn't open the doors until eleven o'clock, and we have had non-stop traffic."

Wanda asked, "Do you need us to do anything?"

David laughed and said, "I wish you could, but we can make it."

Ben exclaimed, "My one arm is pretty good!"

Wanda said, "I can put Ben in the stroller and I can do something to help!"

David pleaded, "If you could give me one hour, that would really help!"

Ben said, "No problem!"

Wanda and Ben stepped right in to help where they could. God allowed baby Ben to sleep for two hours. David and Dee really appreciated the help. They were able to serve most of the customers. There were only ten people left in line.

David said, "Tomorrow, I guess I will be hiring two more people."

Wanda said, "Plan on this heavy traffic into October."

Dee exclaimed, "I hate that I have to go back to the university."

David said, "We agreed that you would finish college, no matter what!"

Dee leaned into David and said, "I know. As soon as I can, I'll be back on Friday."

Everyone laughed.

The café continued to draw large crowds until the middle of November. The reviews were amazing. The local paper did a feature article. The television news channel from Macon stopped by to do an interview in October and November. David was so busy he could not do any catering. Baby Ben continued to grow and bring joy to all. Mary came home for Thanksgiving.

Mom hosted Thanksgiving dinner in the small room at the celebration center. This time there were more guests: Ben, Wanda, baby Ben, David, Dee, Mary, her roommate Eva,

Uncle Robert, Auntie Charlene, Miss Bessie, Mrs. Boatwright, Wanda's parents, Becky and her mother Miss Tammy.

This time Mom suggested that everyone bring something. She would prepare the turkey and ham. The food was not only abundant, but delicious. It was great eating everyone's cooking.

Mom said, "This is the best Thanksgiving ever!"

Everyone agreed.

Uncle Robert said, "God has blessed our families so much this year, we can't help but be grateful."

Auntie Charlene said, "I have never been happier."

Ben said, "Me neither. I'm happy to announce that I have completed five months of rehabilitation. My shoulder is not one hundred percent yet, but it's a good eighty-five percent. I can pick up my son with no problems."

Wanda said, "I'll make sure he continues his exercises at home."

Ben said, "I will not be one hundred percent until I can pick her up again!"

Everyone laughed.

Mrs. Boatwright said, "I'm so thankful to share this holiday with all of you. God has truly blessed me with friendship from your family. I feel the same way as Charlene. I have never been happier. I love my life now. I have purpose and so much love to give."

Everyone applauded.

Mary stood up and said, "That's great, Mrs. Boatwright! I have some great news. As you all know Eva and I went to Spain in October for three weeks. It was great. Before we left the university, Dean White, told us that we had been invited back to Spain for the summer. The exchange program wants us to work there during the summer for eight weeks."

Wanda said, "That's wonderful!"

Mom said, "I thought you would be home for the summer. I don't know what I was thinking!"

Everyone laughed.

David said, "I guess your passport will be filling up soon!"

Ben asked, "Do you need anything?"

Eva said, "No, they are paying our travel expenses, lodging expenses, and paying us what is equivalent to five dollars per hour. I have never made five dollars an hour. I made a list of the places we want to visit. We want to visit Barcelona, Madrid, Grenada, and everywhere else we can squeeze in."

Mary said, "We'll work thirty hours a week. That will give us time to travel."

Eva said excitedly, "Minimum wage is currently $3.35, so we will be making good money. We're very excited."

Mom said, "That's great. At least since you're going together, I won't worry as much."

Eva exclaimed, "That's the same thing my mother said!"

Everyone laughed.

Dad said, "That's a great opportunity. I'm so happy for you."

Momma said, "When I was young, I enjoyed traveling. I got a chance to visit many parts of the United States, but I was never brave enough to even think about international travel."

Dad asked, "Do you still want to go?"

Momma said, "Deep down I do."

Dad said, "Well, let's plan something. What's stopping us?"

Leaning into her husband, Momma exclaimed, "I guess nothing at all!"

Everyone cheered and applauded.

David asked, "When do you think you want to travel?"

Momma said, "Well, now that I can plan it, maybe we can travel during the summer."

David stood up and said, "That sounds nice. I would like to say something."

Everyone put down their fork and gave David their full attention. David took Dee's hand and gently pulled her up. Dee stood next to David.

David said, "I know a lot of you think that I have been slow regarding Dee's and my relationship."

Everyone laughed.

David said, "I can't imagine my life without her. Dee, you know how much I love you."

Dee said, "I do."

David dropped to one knee and asked, "Would you do me the honor of marrying me?"

Dee leaped with joy.

Trying to get her composure, Dee said, "I would love to marry you!"

David slipped the engagement ring on her finger. Everyone applauded and cheered. David hugged Dee and kissed her lovingly.

Smiling Dee said, "I love you David, I always have!"

David said, "Thanks for waiting on me, I love you too!"

Everyone got up from the table to hug the couple.

Momma said excitedly, "Dee, let me see the ring!"

Dee held out her hand.

Momma said, "Wow, this is a very nice ring. It's about two karats, heart shaped diamond, E on the colorless scale, and internally flawless. That's a very, very nice ring!"

Everyone laughed.

9

A STRONG FAMILY BOND

David and Dee set at wedding date of Saturday, December 18, 1982. Dee would be on Christmas Break from college and would have at least three weeks before she went back to class. David and Dee sat down with Uncle Robert to talk about the wedding date.

David said, "I hope the proposal did not come as a surprise to you!"

Uncle Robert said, "No, it didn't! I'm very happy for you both. It's obvious how much you love Dee. Everyone knows how much she loves you. Even before you were a couple."

David said, "Yes sir. The age difference really was holding me back. At first, she was too young. I wanted to wait until she turned eighteen. Then I did not want to stand in the way of her meeting someone else when she went off to college. However, the more I thought about it. I didn't want to lose her to someone else when she went off to college."

Everyone laughed.

Dee smiled and said, "My heart has always belonged to you!"

David pulled her close and said, "We would like to get married December eighteenth. I know she will be in her second year of college. We have discussed this and agreed that she will complete her degree."

Dee said, "Dad, I won't let anything stop me from finishing my degree."

Uncle Robert said, "I believe that. I support your wedding date."

David said, "Of course, we will get married at the celebration center."

Dee said, "We want the wedding to start early. What do you think about eleven o'clock in the morning?"

Uncle Robert said, "That's early!"

David said, "For the honeymoon, we will have to drive. So, I don't want it to be too late when we get on the road."

Uncle Robert said, "That would be fine. Just let me know what you need me to do."

Hugging her dad, Dee said, "Thanks Dad!"

David said, "We really appreciate your support."

Dee said, "The café is doing great!"

Uncle Robert said, "I know. Everyone that comes in the store is talking about it. Charlene said that everyone at the school is talking about it too."

David said, "We're very pleased with the community support. The spaghetti sauce is starting to do really well."

Uncle Robert asked, "Do you want to do any other types of sauces?"

David said, "I'm not sure yet. That's a possibility. The company I'm working with wants me to think about a barbeque sauce. I want to carve out some time to cater. The café has kept me so busy."

Uncle Robert asked, "Have you thought about who would cater your reception?"

Dee exclaimed, "I told him that he has to find someone else. I don't want him cooking and getting married at the same time."

David laughed and said, "I have a friend that I went to culinary school with. I will ask him to do it for me."

Dee exclaimed proudly, "David hired an assistant manager!"

Uncle Robert said, "That's great. You need that."

David said, "Yes sir. I was also thinking if I hire someone now, I will have time to train them well. So, when we go on our honeymoon, I won't have to worry about the café."

Uncle Robert said, "That's great planning."

David said, "I'm also looking for a house, so we will have a place to live when we return from our honeymoon."

Uncle Robert smiled and said, "Sounds like you plan to take great care of my daughter."

David smiled and said, "Yes sir. I do. I love her!"

Mary and Eva were able to convince the university to sponsor a trip to France. The trip was scheduled for March 1982. Mary was very excited. During the summer, she and Eva would be returning to Spain for eight weeks. The family planned to see Mary for three weeks in May. That was only because she had to move out of the dorm, when spring semester was over.

The next few months went by fast. Baby Ben was growing and being loved by all. Ben and Wanda opened the office building. It was a two-story building. There were eight offices upstairs that would be leased to businesses. Ben and Wanda's office was huge. It accommodated two large desks, a sitting area, private restroom, and a kitchenette area.

The daycare center was state of the art. Wanda hired a

director for the daycare facility. She would also be involved in the hiring of each daycare worker. The daycare center was scheduled to open on April 5, 1982. Wanda already had a waiting list of parents that wanted to enrolled their child. Ben and Wanda had a regular meeting scheduled with Timothy Stevens, the accountant.

Ben said, "Mr. Stevens, I know we have been keeping you busy."

Timothy laughed and said, "It's a good busy. I am so proud to be a part of all that you are doing for the city. My job is to abet you and it has brought me great joy."

Wanda said, "We couldn't do it without you!"

Timothy smiled and said, "Well, your portfolio continues to grow. With the two stores, the event center, the sports complex, the car wash, the storage unit, the movie theater, bowling alley, putt-putt golf, the additional land, rental property and the remaining buildings that your grandpa left you, you are now worth fifty-eight million dollars."

Wanda asked, "Does that include all that we have spent and donated?"

Ben said, "In the last two years we have donated so much more in charity and scholarships."

Timothy smiled and said, "Yes, it does. God is blessing. The more you give, the more he gives to you."

Wanda said, "Wow!"

Timothy asked, "Do you have any other ideas or do you want to take a break?"

Ben said, "I have a big idea, but it may be too big."

Timothy laughed and said, "There's no such thing!"

Ben said, "Last year Wanda and I discussed an auditorium for the city. A place where concerts and plays could be held.

High schools could also put on performances and have their graduations there. I am not sure if it will be a money maker!"

Timothy said, "That is a big idea. Let me check to see how much it would cost and how much use is required for it to be a good investment."

Wanda said, "We also plan to talk to Mr. Jennings about selling franchises for the sporting goods store."

Timothy said, "That's a great idea. Royalties would come in regularly and you won't have to do the work."

Ben said, "That's good to hear. As you know David and Dee will be getting married in December. He's looking for a house."

Timothy said, "Well, last year you picked up three more houses to rent. However, there is one that your grandpa already had that is on your street."

Ben asked, "Is it vacant? I thought all of the property had leases."

Timothy said, "It will be vacant in June of this year. If you like, you can put it on the market."

Wanda said, "That would be great. I know David won't accept us giving it to him. We can lower the price so he can get a great house for a great deal."

Timothy said, "We can spruce it up like we did your house."

Ben said, "That's great. I would love for him and Dee to live close by."

Wanda said, "I would like to continue to pick up rental property whenever you can."

Timothy asked, "Would you like to buy in other cities too or just here in Fairville?"

Ben said, "Other neighboring cities!"

Wanda said, "I know that Fairville is growing, but people can't come here if they don't have anywhere to stay."

Ben asked, "Mr. Stevens, what do you think about duplexes or an apartment complex?"

Timothy said, "I think an apartment complex would be fantastic. We purchased some land last year off of Highway 29. Let me talk to Hank about it. We can draft up a plan."

Wanda said, "Mr. Stevens, you have been so helpful to us; we really appreciate it."

Ben said, "We do. I know that we pay you and Mr. Jennings every month for your services. We would like to increase what we pay by ten percent."

Timothy said, "That is extremely generous of you. Your grandpa established an amount that was already very generous."

Wanda said, "However, he did not know we would be working you and Mr. Jennings as much as we are!"

Everyone laughed.

Mary came home in May to drop off her belongings. She was excited about working in Spain for the summer. She spent every day of the three weeks with little Ben. Everywhere she went, she took him with her. If she could not take Ben, she did not go. She tried to teach him to say 'Auntie Mary', he just cooed at her. She was determined to establish a bond with her nephew. She talked to him about everything. When she spoke French, he just laughed.

Dee was happy to be home for the summer. She and Wanda planned the wedding, shopped for dresses, and everything else they needed. David deposited money into Dee's account to pay for the wedding. Uncle Robert was surprised, but also very pleased.

In July, after the rental house had been spruced up. Mr. Stevens told David about the house. David was so excited. He wanted to surprise Dee with the house, so he asked Ben and Wanda to walk through it with him.

As they drove up to the house, David said, "This is a very nice house."

Ben said, "It's a two-story."

Wanda said, "I love the front yard."

David unlocked the front door.

Ben said, "David, this is very nice. The owners have installed new carpet throughout and painted the walls."

David said, "I know. Can you believe the price is $40,000? A brick house like this, in 1982 normally sells for at least $65,000."

Wanda said, "This is a good buy."

David asked, "Do you think something is wrong with it?"

Ben said, "No, I don't. If you like, you can get it inspected to make sure. I think an inspection will cost you about $150."

David said, "OK, I'll do that!"

Wanda said, "It could be that the owner just wants to get rid of some property."

David said, "I like that it's near your house! I think your house is three doors down."

Ben said, "You're right. I love that too!"

Walking through the house, Wanda said, "These look like new appliances."

David said, "I know. The listing said new carpet, new appliances, and freshly painted inside and out."

Ben asked, "Do you like these appliances? You may want a chef's kitchen!"

David said, "I like what they have here. Ben, I don't want to tarry and miss out on it."

Ben asked, "What reservations do you have?"

David said, "I'm sure Dee will like it. It's spacious, there are four bedrooms upstairs. There's even a small study down stairs."

Wanda said, "I saw that. The lot outside looks about

one-fourth of an acre. That's a nice size lot, not huge. It's big enough for a patio set and room for kids to play."

Ben asked, "Is the price holding you back?"

David said, "I have the money to pay for it. I'm trying not to be skeptical. I just can't believe that someone would sell the house at such a reduced price."

Ben said, "Well, it could be a gift from God. This house could have been saved for you."

Elated David acceded, "You're right. I'm going to buy it."

Wanda said, "That's a great decision. When are you going to tell Dee about it?"

David said, "I don't want to keep it from her, but I also want it to be a surprise."

Wanda said, "Ben told me about our house on our honeymoon."

David asked, "Did you like the surprise?"

Wanda smiled and said, "I really did. Ben bought a bedroom set and a dinette set, but left everything else empty so I could decorate it."

David said, "That's a great idea. I'll do the same thing."

Ben said, "David, this is a great house. I believe you and Dee will be very happy here."

David hugged his brother and sister-in-law. He loved his family.

Wanda said, "No matter what, keep it a secret. Be careful where you put the documents. Dee is noisy!"

David laughed and said, "You're right. If she asks, I will tell her that I have our home taken care of."

Ben said, "Great idea!"

Ben and Wanda enjoyed the break they were taking. This break gave them time to focus on little Ben. He was growing so fast. Wanda weaned him from breast milk. He was very smart and starting to walk. He already had four teeth. They had a big family celebration for his first birthday at the house. Everyone had a great time.

Mrs. Boatwright said, "Ben! Wanda! You're doing a great job with baby Ben!"

Wanda said, "Thank you. He's pure joy!"

Smiling Ben said, "We try hard."

Mrs. Boatwright asked, "Do you want more?"

Ben said, "Yes, ma'am we do."

Mrs. Boatwright said, "I'm glad. You both have so much love to give. Your mother has been talking to me about Jesus. I gave my life to Christ on yesterday when we were in the park."

Wanda said, "That's wonderful."

Ben said, "I'm so glad."

Mrs. Boatwright said, "I am too. You moving across the street has changed my life. I'm so grateful to God for giving me another chance to get it right."

Wanda said, "We are too!"

Ben said, "Mrs. Boatwright, I just wanted to give you a heads up. The house that the Everette Family lived in down the street is for sale."

Mrs. Boatwright said, "I know. I already started praying that whoever moves in will be good for our neighborhood."

Wanda smiled and said, "I will join you in that prayer!"

Mary was sad that she missed the birthday party. She returned from Spain two weeks before classes started in August. She looked different. She was slimmer and more confident. She enjoyed working at the Student Exchange and traveling all over Spain.

Mary said, "I had a great time. They asked me if I wanted to do it again next summer."

Mom asked, "Do you?"

Mary said, "I'm not sure. I would like to go somewhere different next summer. That would be my last summer before graduation."

Mom said, "I can't believe you will be a junior this fall. My, how time flies!"

Mary said, "I can't believe it either. I need to figure out exactly what I want to do."

Ben asked, "Do you want to get your master's degree?"

Mary said, "I thought about it. I'm not sure."

Ben said, "I do know that it's easier to go ahead and get it. Once you start working it's harder to make time for it."

Mary said, "That's good information, Thanks!"

Mom asked, "Do you need anything for school?"

Mary said, "No! Eva will be my roommate again. Ben keeps money in my bank account, so if I need anything I can just buy it."

Mom said, "Ben, I didn't know you still did that!"

Ben said, "Yes, ma'am. I check her account about once a quarter, if I think it's too low. I put some in it!"

Mom said, "Ben, you take such good care of our family. I'm so proud of the man you have become."

Ben smiled and hugged his mother tightly.

He said, "I guess you raised me right!"

Everything was on track for the wedding. Dee could focus on her classes during the fall semester. The café was doing well. It had been open almost a year. No matter how much David prepped, it was barely enough for the day. People from other cities were coming to Fairville to eat at the café. There was no need to advertise. The television station in Macon did a follow up story on the café. Customers were very pleased. He also had regular cake orders. Business was booming.

David had little time for catering. Mom was struggling to

find a good cater that would come to Fairville. David contacted some of his classmates to see if they were interested. James Strong graduated with David, he was very interested. He had been working at a restaurant in Atlanta, but wanted something different. James visited Fairville on the first weekend in August.

He really liked Fairville and he loved the event center. Mom explained to him that he would not be working for the event center, but that people would hire him directly. James was very impressed with what he saw. He planned to relocate to Fairville in September.

David said, "I'm so glad that you like it here."

James said, "What's not to like! The event center is awesome. The city is very comforting! Congratulations, you have a great café."

David said, "Thanks! Fairville is growing, so if you are interested in opening your own place. This is the place to do it!"

James said, "That's a great idea. I'm from a small town not too far from here."

David said, "I didn't know that. Where?"

James said, "Butler, Georgia! It's about two hours from here."

David asked, "Do you still have family there?"

James said, "I have some cousins. My parents died before I went to culinary school."

David said, "I'm sorry. Don't you have an older brother?"

James said, "Yes, he lives in Atlanta. It was good to spend time with him these last five years."

David said, "I'm happy to be back home with my family. I missed them!"

James exclaimed, "Your sister, Mary! She's beautiful."

David said, "Mary has a lot going for her. She's very intelligent and very focused."

James said, "I'm sure she is!"

David said, "She leaves in a couple of days. She will be starting her junior year at the University of Georgia."

James said, "That's impressive. Did I misunderstand or did she say that she was in Spain for the summer?"

David said, "That's what she said. She worked there for eight weeks. She got a chance to travel. She's also a polyglot."

James asked, "What is a polyglot?"

David laughed and said, "A polyglot is someone who speaks multiple languages. Mary speaks Spanish and French fluently."

James asked, "Is she seeing anyone?"

David said, "No, not many guys measure up to what she is looking for!"

Shaking his head James said, "I'm sure they don't!"

It was hard for Mary to leave Fairville this time. She missed her family. Being away for the summer showed her just how much. She vowed to come home more this year. She did not want little Ben to not know his Auntie Mary.

Mr. Jennings advertised that franchises were available for Cason's Sporting Goods. One man from Atlanta was very interested. Timothy Stevens was working on the plan to build an apartment complex. Mr. Jennings was also working with the city to see if an auditorium would be of interest.

Ben and Wanda continued to fill in when the manager was not available at either of the two stores. They also helped out during personnel shortages.

Ben said, "This week we need to make a trip to audit the store in Macon."

Wanda asked, "OK, would you like to stay overnight?"

Ben said, "That's a great idea!"

Wanda suggested, "Let's leave Ben with Mrs. Boatwright!"

Ben said, "That's fine. We'll only be gone for one night."

Wanda said, "I've been thinking. I want to stop taking birth control."

Concerned Ben asked, "Are you OK? Are you having any side effects?"

Wanda said, "Oh no! I was just thinking, Ben is fifteen months now. It may take a few months for me to conceive."

Ben said, "OK! I know how happy you are to be at your pre-baby weight."

Wanda laughed and said, "Yes, that's true. If I'm gaining weight for a good cause, I'm OK with it."

Ben laughed and said, "Babies are always a good cause!"

Wanda said, "OK, I did not take my pill this morning. So, I won't take anymore until after we have another child."

Ben smiled and said, "I love you very much!"

Wanda pulled him close and said, "I love you more!"

10

SAVED FOR EACH OTHER

Dee drove home every Friday to see David and help with the café. She was doing very well in her classes. She needed to decide about her classes for spring semester. She would be married to the love of her life then; she did not want to stay in the dorm. However, she could not commute one and a half hours three days a week either. After talking to David, they decided that she would continue to live in the dorm. After her last class on Friday, she would drive home for the weekend.

David said, "I know that you don't want to stay in the dorm, but I think this is the best plan."

Dee said, "I know. I'll take three classes on Tuesday and Thursday, and two classes on Monday, Wednesday, and Friday. Hopefully, I can be on the road to come home on Friday by 11:30 in the morning."

David said, "That sounds great."

Dee said, "I don't want to delay my degree. I want to get this over!"

David laughed.

Dee said, "I love you David!"

David said, "I love you too!"

Dee said, "I have been thinking about birth control. As you know, I'm still a virgin. Since I have to finish this degree, I think that we should plan our family."

David said, "I thought about that too!"

Dee said, "So, do you agree that I should see a doctor and get a prescription for birth control pills."

David said, "I do. As much as I want to have children with you, they'll have to wait."

Dee said, "David, I never asked you. Have you been with other women before?"

David smiled and said, "No, I haven't. I wanted to wait until I got married."

Dee said, "Deep down I knew that!"

David smiled and said, "So, I guess we can both figure it out together!"

Dee smiled and said, "I like that idea! Considering all of the women in Atlanta, I'm somewhat surprised."

David said, "You're right the women are abundant in Atlanta. Some are also very promiscuous. I decided back in high school that if I was going to be intimate with someone, I had to be ready to marry them. Then I decided, that I would wait until I got married."

Dee said, "My decision was easy. I never wanted to be with anyone but you. A lot of guys made passes at me and asked me out in high school. They never measured up to what I saw in you."

David pulled her closed and kissed her lovingly.

Dee smiled and said, "I look forward to the honeymoon!"

David laughed and asked, "Do you want to know where we're going or do you want it to be a surprise?"

Dee said, "I want it to be a surprise. Since it will be winter time, I know what to pack!"

David smiled and said, "Don't pack too much!"

Dee laughed!

David said, "I have also been thinking that you need a car."

Dee smiled and said, "Wanda's car has been doing fine. I haven't had any major problems since you replaced the alternator last month."

David said, "Well, I have enough money saved. I want to buy you a car. Do you want to buy it now or buy it for the wedding?"

Dee leaped with joy. Then she tried to regain her composure.

She said, "I like that idea. Are you sure, we can afford it?"

David said, "Yes, I've been saving all of my spaghetti sauce money and the café is doing very well."

Dee said, "Well, it's October now. Let's get it for the wedding unless something happens to Wanda's car."

David said, "That's a great plan. Do you want me to surprise you or do you want to pick it out?"

Dee exclaimed, "I want to pick it out!"

David laughed and said, "Tomorrow, I plan to clean your car before you go back."

Dee smiled and said, "David, you're spoiling me!"

David said, "I know. You want me to stop!"

Dee said, "No! I guess we'll spoil each other."

David said, "I like that. I don't want you to regret waiting for me."

Dee said, "I can't imagine that!"

Mary continued to thrive at the university. She and Eva were good friends. One day she was leaving class in the Cultural Studies building, Dean White stopped her.

Dean White asked, "Mary, do you have time to talk for a minute?"

Mary smiled and said, "Yes, sir. I finished all of my classes for the day."

Dean White said, "Please, step into my office."

Mary walked into the office and took a seat.

Dean White said, "Mary, I have an opportunity that I think would be great for you."

Mary asked, "What type of opportunity?"

Dean White said, "You're familiar with our university television station. Currently, our department does not have a presence. I want to create a broadcast and I want you to be our spokesperson."

Mary asked, "Spokesperson?"

Dean White said, "I want to create a show where you interview Cultural Studies students. I think your personality and intelligence will provide the x-factor that we need. Would you be interested?"

Surprised Mary said, "I have never done anything like that before."

Dean White said, "You're very captivating, tenacious, and gregarious. I think you will do well in this role. I really want you to consider it and not abandon the idea, because it is something new."

Mary asked, "How often will we record a broadcast?"

Dean White said, "I was thinking at least twice a month. After we build up a following, we could expand it to weekly."

Mary said, "This is a great opportunity. I am interested. Would I have any say on who we interviewed or segments that we did?"

Dean White said, "Of course. There will be some mandatory

items that we will have to cover, but I am interested in your opinion and ideas."

Mary asked, "When would this start?"

Dean White said, "Well, I have already established a ground crew. We can use the campus studio to record. Today is Tuesday, I was hoping we can record our first segment by Saturday."

Mary said, "That's quick. Do you have ideas for the first segment?"

Dean White said, "I do. I have three students you can interview and some announcements that need to be made."

Mary said, "I need to do some research. I don't know anything."

Dean White said, "The studio is accustomed to doing these broadcasts all the time. I told Faye Evans about you. All you have to do is stop by her office and she will guide you. I will contact the three students and have them stop by too."

Smiling Mary said, "This is exciting, but also very scary!"

Dean White said, "I have the utmost confidence in you. I know that it will be a great show."

Mary asked, "Do you think Miss Evans will talk to me today?"

Dean White saw that Mary was nervous.

He said, "I am sure she will. Relax! I feel very good about this project!"

Mary stood up and said, "Thank you for considering me. I will do my best!"

Dean White smiled and said, "If you do your best, I am sure the broadcast will be great!"

Dean White was right. Mary's broadcast was great. She was a natural. It was kismet. She was very entertaining. She asked thoughtful and intelligent questions. She received rave reviews.

Dean White was very pleased. Mary asked Eva to help with the production. Eva was ecstatic. She learned so much from watching Mary. Mary was very poised and professional. People thought she had been doing this all of her life.

After the second broadcast, they started recording every week. Mary was very pleased. Miss Evans trained her on outfit selection, colors, makeup, hair, and transitioning from one subject to another.

Some of Mary's guests did not speak English well. If they spoke Spanish or French, she was able to interpret their native language and relay to the audience their response. Mary's broadcast was aired three different times throughout the day. University students, instructors, and staff were very impressed. Mary had found her calling. Her family was very proud of her.

The next few weeks flew by. Everyone was preparing for David and Dee's wedding. Reverend King would officiate the ceremony, unless something happened. Judge Jennings was invited to the wedding just in case. Dee chose a burgundy 1983 Chevrolet Cavalier. It was fully loaded with front wheel drive, AC, cruise control, leather seats, power windows, and automatic transmission. One of Ben's job as the best man was to park the car in the front of the celebration center after the wedding and attach a sign that said 'just married' on the back.

Dee would have three bride's maids: Wanda, Mary, and Pam. For his groomsmen David selected Ben, James, and Jeff, his friend from church.

The women at the church threw Dee a wedding shower. She was showered with love and gifts. Everyone had a great time. David hung out with his groomsmen at the bowling alley. They had so much fun. He loved his brother, his future father in law, and his friends. After bowling they all went to get a haircut together. He knew that Grandpa would be proud of him.

James Strong had been doing a great job catering at the event center. The customers were very pleased. He was happy with the money he was making. He would cater the rehearsal dinner and reception. Dee wanted a light rehearsal dinner, nothing heavy. On Friday night before the wedding, the rehearsal and dinner went well. Most of the same people that attended Ben and Wanda's wedding were invited to David and Dee's wedding. Everyone was excited.

Saturday morning, December 18, 1982, had finally arrived. David went for a run to calm his nerves. He arrived at the church at nine o'clock that morning. He saw Dee's car when he drove up. He took the time to say a prayer. He thanked God for saving Dee for him. He loved her very much. He thanked God for his businesses and the ability to take care of his future family. He asked God for wisdom to help him make the right decisions as he and Dee lived the rest of their lives. Revered King was in the event center already.

Shocked David said, "Reverend King, you're here already!"

Reverend King smiled and said, "I did not want you to worry. I feel good. It's going to be a great celebration today."

David laughed and said, "Thank you! I'm excited."

Reverend King said, "I know I told you this already, but you and Dee make a beautiful couple."

David smiled and said, "Thank you. I love her very much!"

Reverend King laughed and said, "Everyone knows how she feels about you!"

The groomsmen got dressed and were waiting for the ceremony to start. Mom knocked on the door. David opened the door and smiled.

Mom asked, "Is everyone ready?"

David said, "Yes ma'am, we're ready. Is Dee OK?"

Mom said, "She's fine. She looks beautiful."

David said, "I know she does."

Mom asked, "Are you nervous?"

David said, "No ma'am, I'm not. I'm ready. I have no reservations at all."

Mom hugged her son and said, "It should only be a few minutes. Everyone is in place. The ballroom is full. I think some people brought a friend!"

David laughed and said, "I asked James to prepare enough food for two-hundred and twenty-five people!"

Mom laughed and went to check on Dee. When she opened the door, Dee was standing in the middle of the room.

Mom exclaimed, "Dee, you look beautiful!"

Dee smiled and said, "Thank you so much!"

Mom asked, "Are you nervous?"

Dee smiled and said, "No ma'am. I've imagined this wedding since I was in the fifth grade."

Everyone laughed.

Mom said, "Well, we should be starting soon."

David and his groomsmen took their place next to the wedding arch. David wore a white tuxedo with a mauve bow tie and cummerbund. His groomsmen wore white tuxedo coats with black pants and matching bow ties and cummerbunds. The wedding arch was decorated beautifully with mauve and white flowers. The bridesmaids' dresses were mauve with shoes dyed to match. Dee wore a white wedding gown with a sweetheart neckline. The dress had spaghetti straps. The train was only about twelve inches. It was a simple dress that complimented her hour glass figure. Her veil did not cover her face. She wore her hair up in a twist with curls framing her face. There was no flower girl or ring bearer. Little Ben was only seventeen months, he was not ready to walk down the aisle by himself. During the ceremony, Mrs. Boatwright held Ben. Ben adored her. The church quartet sang beautifully.

As the bridesmaids were walking down the aisle, David thought about how he had tried to avoid Dee over the years. He laughed at himself. He thanked God for not letting her give up on him. When Dee appeared at the back of the room, David's heart skipped a beat. She looked beautiful. Everyone stood up as she walked down the aisle.

David could not stop smiling. He was so thankful. When she took her place next to him, he wanted to just grab her. He remained calm. Reverend King spoke beautifully about their childhood and how happy he was to see them together. They exchanged vows. They decided to wear simple bands of gold. David slipped the ring on her finger and smiled. You could hear a pin drop, everyone was so quiet even little Ben. He occupied himself with his teething ring.

When Reverend King announced that you may now kiss your bride, David did not want to appear too eager. He did not have to, Dee quickly grabbed him. Everyone laughed.

David escorted his beautiful wife to the back of the room and then hugged her tightly and kissed her passionately. Mom made the announcement that pictures needed to be taken and for the audience to please be patient.

Pictures were taken quickly. The bridal table was served. David did not want to let go of Dee's hand. James had prepared prime rib and chicken breast with a rosemary cream sauce. David made the wedding cakes. He made a red velvet and a lemon one. Both cakes were three tiers, beautifully decorated. They were works of art. Everyone commented that they would order their future wedding cake from him.

There were no problems during the wedding and reception.

Everything went according to plan. Miss Bessie kept everything on track. David and Dee walked around to each table thanking the guests for coming. The photographer took pictures of the couple at every table. The videographer recorded everything.

Ben suggested for David to pick a longer song for his first dance with Dee. David chose a longer song, but it was still too short. After their dance, David danced with his mother and Dee danced with her dad. It was a beautiful sight.

Then the floor was open to all who wanted to dance. James could not wait to ask Mary to dance. Mary graciously accepted the invitation. Every other single guy in the room also asked Mary to dance. She danced until she did not want to dance any more. Ben danced with Wanda several times. They still danced like no one else was in the room.

Wanda said, "Ben, I love you. You've been a great husband to me and a wonderful father to our son."

Ben said, "Thanks, I love you too!"

Wanda said, "I have some news that I have to tell you, but I don't want you to say anything yet. This is David's and Dee's day."

Ben stopped dancing and looked at his wife.

Wanda smiled and said, "I'm pregnant!"

With a one hundred percent healed shoulder Ben picked up his wife, twirled her around, and then hugged her tightly.

Wanda laughed and said, "I guess you didn't say anything!"

Smiling Ben whispered, "Wait until David and Dee leave. I will make a big announcement!"

Wanda smiled while Ben twirled her around, he then pulled her close to continue dancing. Finally, it was time for David and Dee to change clothes. The ushers passed out a small gift to everyone with a laced bundle of rice. The guests found in the box a beautiful Christmas ornament with a picture of David and Dee. At the bottom was 'David and Dee Davis, December 18, 1982'. It was a beautiful keepsake.

When the couple reappeared before the crowd, everyone applauded. Dee wore a beautiful white laced dress with one-inch white heels. The dress length was right above her knee. David wore a long sleeved, white shirt with a pair of burgundy slacks. They looked very nice.

David said, "We want to thank you for coming out to celebrate with us today."

Dee said, "We hope you enjoy our small token of love."

David said, "We're off to Savannah. Don't expect us back until after the New Year."

Everyone laughed.

Mom walked in front of the room and hugged her son and new daughter in law. The ushers ushered the guests out so they could throw rice at the couple.

Mom said, "I'm so proud of you both. I love you!"

David said, "Thanks Mom, for everything!"

Mom said, "It has been my pleasure raising you."

Uncle Robert hugged his daughter and said, "Dee, you knew what you wanted and you did not give up. I'm so proud of you. You make good choices."

Dee was so happy that tears were rolling down her face. David and Dee made their way through the crowd, when they got outside the new 1983 Chevrolet Cavalier was waiting for them. Everyone threw rice. David hugged his family one more time, then opened the car door for his beautiful bride.

As they got in the car to drive away, David said, "Is Savannah OK with you? If not, we can go somewhere else."

Dee smiled and said, "I've always wanted to go to Savannah. I love you David."

Leaning over to kiss her one more time, David said, "I love you too!"

As the car drove away, the guests started to go back inside. People were busy talking and gathering their things.

Ben took the microphone and said, "Thank you again for helping us celebrate David and Dee. I would also like to make an announcement. My beautiful wife just informed me that we are expecting again! Our family is growing!"

Everyone applauded. Everyone could not wait to congratulate the couple.

To be continued…

Continue on this amazing journey with Ben as he discovers all that God has saved for him. Order today:

Book 1	Saved for Ben	ISBN 978-1-6642-6888-3
Book 2	Saved for Ben: The College Years	ISBN 978-1-6642-6892-0
Book 3	Saved for Ben: Ben and Wanda	ISBN 978-1-6642-6895-1
Book 4	Saved for Ben: The Legacy	ISBN 978-1-6642-6898-2

Stay tuned for the continuing saga!

Printed in the United States
by Baker & Taylor Publisher Services